Wavelength

a novel

Angus Morrison

Published by Waldorf Publishing
2140 Hall Johnson Road
#102-345
Grapevine, Texas 76051
www.WaldorfPublishing.com

Wavelength

ISBN: 978-1-944244-73-6
Library of Congress Control Number: 2015957007

Printed in Canada

There's not much dignity in dying in the bathtub, but that's where they found him—naked, wet, and full of electricity.

To the coroner, it could have been just another lump of flesh laid out on a metal slab waiting to be cut up and exposed for what it was—essentially a bucket of water with carbon, nitrogen, hydrogen, tin, lead, copper, tungsten, sulfur, sodium, germanium, and a cocktail of 48 other elements. But he knew this guy. Well, he didn't really *know* him, he knew *of* him, from the headlines.

"Somebody murdered him. Right, doctor?" the detective asked, making a face at the sight of the clammy body.

"Hard to say, monsieur. No marks point to a struggle."

"You mean he hugged his radio and fried himself in 12 inches of water? That's talent."

"Was there any sign of forced entry?"

"No."

"Painful way to relieve oneself of this world, you know."

"What is, doctor?"

"Electrocution. Kind of like parboiling from the inside out."

"What happens?"

"Well, the combination of water from the tub and salt in the body cause the electricity to course through you, which causes painful muscle contractions, burning, and swelling of the organs because of the rapid rise in body temperature. A small amount of electricity also enters the brain, but because there is no massive coagulation necrosis of tissue the brain doesn't cease to function instantaneously. The electricity that does penetrate the brain activates those regions that produce intense feelings of fear, dread, and pain. The real cause of death is normally laryngeal asphyxia due to muscle contraction of the larynx, or general asphyxia due to the muscle contraction of the lungs, or ventricular fibrillation of the heart. Bottom line: they know what's going on before they die."

"Why do people do it, doc?"

"Kill themselves? Hard to say. For many of them, it comes down to science—chemical imbalance, that sort of thing. Others just don't want to wake up in the morning. Then there are those people who are shamed into doing it."

"That what happened to him?"

"Probably."

"I didn't think that shame was part of their DNA—guys like him."

"He obviously had a good dose of it, enough to do himself in."

"But he wasn't the one who brought that company down."

"No, monsieur, but he played the game. He compromised himself just like the rest of them. Probably couldn't bear it anymore, which is why he brought his radio in the bath with him. That is, of course, assuming that it was he who did that."

"I thought you said it was suicide?"

"No, I said that there were no signs of struggle on the body, nor does there seem to have been a forced entry. I can't prove that he was murdered. Therefore, I've got to tag him as a probable suicide. At least, he didn't slit his wrists or put a rifle in his mouth. That's always messy."

"You're a real softy, aren't you, Doc?"

Part I
Chapter 1
(2004)

The hot wash of the stage lights had no effect on Aaron Cannondale. He was on. He could feel his connection with the audience building. It was as if he'd thrown them a lifeline and they were clamoring to be pulled in:

"… On July 4, 1776, King George III wrote the following entry in his diary: 'nothing of importance happened today.'

"That's because he had no idea that a group of men 3,000 miles away in Philadelphia had just declared their independence from the British Crown. I bet the fair king wished he'd had a television, or a telegraph, or a radio ... anything that would have connected him to the rest of the world a bit more quickly. Even today, a lot of people still wish they had such outlets. Half of the world still lives on $1 a day. Half of the world has yet to make its first phone call. As immediate as the world has become, plenty of places are still in the dark. But that's changing … We sit on the eve of a new frontier …"

Aaron noticed a portly fellow in the front row hanging on every word. That's how he wanted them—mesmerized, hypnotized, his.

"The digital railroad tracks of the future continue to be set in place as we speak. Tremendous progress has been made in getting information from A to B quicker than ever before. But it's not good enough. Those

**without cable modems or DSL lines—the majority—still
endure the pain of sluggish email, and stalled-out
Internet connections and ten-minute waits for our
browsers to load. Would any of us put up with this kind
of shoddy service from our cars?"**

Hayden Campbell, Aaron's speechwriter, sat in the
back of the UN central chamber, his lips silently syncing
the words coming out of his client's mouth—the sixth
richest man in the world. Aaron paced around the stage now,
just as Hayden had instructed him. Hayden liked that Aaron
listened to his advice. He appreciated that Aaron
remembered his pointers, like the fact that 70% of every
speech was visual. This was the way a speech giver and
speechwriter were supposed to work, a symbiotic
relationship between pen and mouth. There was trust and
mutual admiration for their respective abilities.

Aaron wasn't like the others Hayden had served. There
had been clients—humorless clients—who pulled 14-hour
days at the office, who didn't know their children, who
walked around like modern-day Atlases, boldly trying to
support the weight of the world with some self-delusional
notion that they, or anyone for that matter, were actually
equipped to do so. His last client, the head of a major oil
company, fell into that category. The executive had been a
complete disappointment—a guy whose arrogance often
caused him to make bad decisions—one of those dangerous
kinds of men who, having read the Cliff Notes version of
The Prince, were under the impression that they understood

how to play that game, even though they failed to grasp that running a company with shareholders was considerably different than running a fiefdom with armies.

Hayden had been hesitant when the client recommended him to Cannondale. He assumed it would be more of the same, but the two men couldn't have been more different.

Then there were the other clients—ruffians who dealt with triads and metaphors the way a wrestler might manhandle a porcelain figurine. And there were the terrified, the ones who were so afraid of getting up in front of an audience that the only way they could deny that fear was to attack Hayden by questioning his research, or his sources, or his ideas.

In the late '90s, when technology temporarily replaced religion and the word "genius" was thrown around loosely, Hayden had found himself working for a particularly untalented speaker—good executive, bad speaker. Their first trip together was to Atlanta. When they arrived at the hotel lobby, the executive pulled him aside. Hayden thought the man was going to ask him to add something to the speech or put the text in a larger font. Instead, the executive asked Hayden to run out to the airport to pick up his lost luggage. Hayden had just started out. He needed the money, and the reference. So he picked up the monogrammed bag and returned to the hotel ballroom to catch the last few minutes of the executive's mediocre delivery. Hayden gave the bag to the guy's secretary backstage and then camped out in the green room.

The man was bad, real bad, but to Hayden's immediate right sat a medieval-sized pewter bowl of peeled shrimp. It was full when Hayden got to it; it was practically empty by the time the two or three lobotomized souls in the audience who actually seemed to like the speech began to clap. Hayden slipped out the back and grabbed a cab to the airport. He relished the thought of the executive looking around for him after the talk, eagerly waiting to be regaled by the kind of ass sniffing that previous speechwriters had afforded him over the course of his career.

Sure, Hayden's new client Aaron Cannondale was as arrogant as they came, but somehow he carried it. His ego wasn't too large to listen or to learn. He valued words. He understood that putting them together just the right way was like having a backstage pass to people's hearts and minds. The guy just got it.

Aaron's inflection was perfect now. His body language was strong. Eye contact was good. He owned the oxygen in the room. The venue was a UN-sponsored conference on closing the digital divide. People were still talking about the "haves and have-nots." Aaron had balked at making an appearance; "too much on my plate," he'd said. But Hayden had talked him into it. A couple of other headline CEOs were there. It wouldn't have looked right if Aaron had missed it.

It was a time of reckoning. The technology industry had been battered around the head. CEOs and CFOs were getting hauled up before grand juries and Senate committee chairmen to answer for accounting gimmickry. Under pressure to move quickly against corporate corruption, a piece of legislation, the Sarbanes-Oxley Act, had rocketed through Congress in 2002. The costs to publicly traded companies were now in the billions. Small and medium-sized businesses were beginning to list overseas instead of in the States. Rounding errors carried the threat of prison sentences. U.S. corporations, paralyzed by fear, sat on their cash, too timid to invest.

Value investors, who were once ridiculed as conservative stegosauruses, were enjoying telling people "I told you so." In the mid-90s, the Telecom Act had opened the floodgates of competition. It had turned a meat and potatoes industry like telecom into a porterhouse of profits. The pioneers had been an odd mix of entrepreneurs: guys who used to climb telephone poles, owners of AM radio stations, construction company foremen, used car salesmen, and high school gym teachers. Each wanted to be the Cornelius Vanderbilt of his time. They had formed their companies with a goal: to build the fiber-optic railroad tracks that would allow people to send huge quantities of data over the Internet.

Competition turned into desperation, and a healthy number of these Vanderbilts were now either on their way to jail or just getting out, but the dream of building high-tech railroad tracks was still there. It was still a crowded arena, one that couldn't help but cannibalize itself. And somewhere in the ugliness, Aaron Cannondale saw opportunity. It wasn't his normal line of business, but it was one that he had told Hayden on a number of occasions he was determined to enter, given the right circumstance.

"The world deserves unlimited bandwidth. It is our collective destiny. I know that some of you doubt that unlimited bandwidth will truly close the digital divide. 'More of the same,' you say. Those who can pay will get the perks. And to a certain degree, you are right, at least in the early stages. But it doesn't have to continue that way. "

Hayden could see Aaron working up to his close. "Pause for effect, Aaron," he said to himself. Like clockwork, Aaron paused, putting on his trademark look of sincerity.

"Let me leave you with this: Working together, we can one day make unlimited bandwidth a reality. Working together, we can ensure that the 'haves' bring the 'have-nots' along with them. Working together—business and government, side-by-side—we may just do some good. "Thank you."**

"Wait for it, Aaron. Good," Hayden whispered. "Applause. Excellent."

Aaron knew he had a gift, and he wasn't shy about using it. The key was unbridled confidence, poise, and a knack for theatrics. He didn't try to do a 100-yard dash to the closing either, as most people did when they gave a speech. Then there was the photographic memory. Hayden could provide him with a speech on the plane and let him disappear for a while to get into the zone. By the time the plane landed he'd find Aaron somewhere in the back doing a crossword puzzle, the speech entirely in his head.

Aaron shook hands with the UN crowd and made his way to the exit. Hayden did his normal thing of slipping out a side door to let his client bask in the afterglow. It was part of a speechwriter's shtick: make your guy look like a rock star, and then get lost.

Hayden's path to speechwriting had been circuitous. He had studied computer science and physics at Cambridge. He was also fluent in Arabic. He had spent time in Morocco and promised himself that he would go back when he could no longer smell the place in his mind—a promise he had long since broken.

Hayden met Aaron at the black town car waiting outside. The New York sun pounded away at the road like an invisible sledgehammer. It was different from the mild sun Hayden had woken up to a day earlier in Salt Lake City, home of Aaron's company, Lyrical. The light was different in New York—somehow more vibrant, more blue. Light was important to Hayden. It helped define a place, or a face, or an event. To him, if light were a word it would be a modifier that turned a perfectly bland sentence into something memorable. Light was also the great rationalizer. It could make an ugly girl look half-decent. It could turn the facade of a decaying building into a wonderland of images. It could seduce you into seeing something that wasn't there, or seeing too much in something basic. Everything was wholly dependent on what kind of light you viewed it in.

"Well, my friend, what did you think?"

"You did well, Aaron. Very well."

"Don't sugarcoat it, Hayden. I must have fucked *something* up?"

"Now that you mention it, you could have paused longer at your kicker."

"Uh huh."

"And you raced through the first two minutes. 'Gotta slow down."

"You're right. Did you see them? No sipping the Kool-Aid today, Hayden. They gulped it down. It was so fresh, Hayden, so original. 'Mr. Original,' that's what you are."

"You were very, very good, Aaron."

They climbed into the back of the car for the ride out to Teterboro. Three years after 9/11 the film reel of lower Manhattan on fire continued to quietly play in the minds of the city's inhabitants—at work, at home, looking out the window of a cross-town bus—but the numbness was gone. In its place was a collective desire to return to good times, times like the great technology wave. It had been a time of dirty Ketel One martinis, black clothing, and new fathers puffing Cohibas as they strolled their infants through Central Park. New Yorkers wanted something like that again. New York was different now, but it would always remember how to make money. It certainly wasn't going to curl up or go fetal, not if Aaron Cannondale had anything to do with it.

Aaron immediately got on the cell phone.

"Lisa, any messages? Right ... uh, huh ... okay ... fuck him ... confirm it ... why? ... who? ... right ... I love it ... change it to the 14th ... can't do that tonight ... right ...tell Nichols that I want him to follow up ... exactly ... turquoise."

Hayden hated cell phones. To him, they were one of the culprits responsible for the decline of the art of conversation. They encouraged a truncated form of the English language that left him feeling as malnourished as the emptiness that set in after polishing off a bag of Cheetos. He decided to get some reading done while Aaron was on the phone.

Hayden opened a manila folder labeled "Speech Fodder" which contained articles that he regularly clipped from newspapers. They covered random topics: an article on the economics of semiconductors, another on AIDS research in Africa, an obituary of Charles K. Johnson, the founder of the Flat Earth Society; a history of the oyster in New York, a discussion on international tariffs, an interpretation of David Hume's "An Enquiry Concerning Human Understanding," and some lines from Thomas Hobbes on the concept of common wealth. There was no rhyme or reason to what he collected; he just knew that at some point he'd work it into a speech.

One article from the *Wall Street Journal* caught his

attention. It was about the Global Positioning System—the constellation of 24 satellites that sit in geosynchronous orbit above the Earth beaming radio signals to the U.S. military, shippers, truckers, hikers, and rental cars. The article pointed out that the signal coming from the satellites, which had to travel 11,000 miles, was so weak that by the time it arrived on Earth; a single Christmas tree light was about 1,000 times as bright. The article went on to say that the signal could essentially be altered by anyone possessing a jamming device that they could get off of the Internet for $40.

"A Christmas tree light," Hayden mumbled to himself in amazement.

"What's that, my friend?" Aaron said, cupping the receiver of his cell phone.

"Nothing. Just talking to myself, Aaron."

"Don't do that."

Chapter 2

Rebecca's is the kind of place where you pay $25 for an egg salad sandwich and a bottle of root beer. But to the inhabitants of Southampton, Long Island, it's just their general store.

Rebecca's reminded Jack Braun of McMillan's in Michigan's Upper Peninsula because of the décor—spartan walls, fresh produce, homemade dills, and tins of beans neatly stacked on pine shelves. Aside from the prices, everything else was pretty much the same—people coming in to pick up their daily newspapers, the owner's daughter behind the counter, an American flag waving out front.

Jack had fled Michigan a long time ago. He was Wall Street now. He had always yearned to leave the simple folk behind, somehow sensing there was more to life than eating Dinty Moore stew out of the can while ice fishing. When he got the math scholarship to Princeton, he took it, thanked his parents, and never looked back. And he never once made apologies for what he now had.

Funny thing, jealousy. That's what he sensed on the rare occasions when he went back to Michigan to check up on his parents. He had money, cars, a house in the Hamptons, a $6 million apartment in Manhattan, and a couple of horses that he raced, the sort of things that men and women back home only saw in movies or talked about derisively over cups of strong black coffee in the diner. He was living the American Dream, but it wasn't good enough for them. They still found a way to make him feel inadequate, to let him know that the secret to happiness wasn't actually in attaining the things you wanted, but rather in the dreaming and the praying and the hoping that if you were good enough and God-fearing enough, you'd find something special in your stocking one day.

Bullshit. That's what it was. Simple-minded, backwater bullshit. If there was one thing that he knew he had going for him that those cowards back at home didn't, it was that he tried to limit the amount of time he spent dreaming. He preferred action. And as a telecom analyst in the mid-to-late '90s, that's what he got. When he started, they paid him $250,000 a year. At the height of the party, he was getting $10 million a year before bonus. They fired him after the telecom meltdown, said he was getting "too close" to the companies he followed. The real reason was that he was expensive and that he had become too much of a poster child for an era that they wanted to put behind them.

When they let him go, he took a year off to travel the world in his plane. Along the way, he picked up an assortment of '90s superheroes doing the same thing. In Norway, it was the former general counsel for an online property that provided answers to random questions posed by users. In Kathmandu, he trekked with the former head of marketing for an online grocery company. He had a memorable dinner with the former head of sales for a clothing dot.com in Bangkok and climbed part of Mt. Kilimanjaro with early investors in a company that delivered videos and snacks to your door. When he got to the Okavango Delta in Botswana, a place where he thought he could soak up the silence, he stumbled upon what felt like a summer camp for dot.com dropouts.

His return to the States was lonely. Friends were gone or hiding in offline leper caves. That said, it all seemed a prelude to him. Yes, he had gotten dinged like the rest of them, but he wasn't staying down. He was now an analyst at Teestone Financial covering computer software and networking. His reports were gaining a following. He was good with words in a way that other analysts were not. That year back in college doing editorials for *The Daily Princetonian* had paid off. The ability to write was still a differentiator in an industry consumed with figures. Institutional holders bought and sold millions of dollars based on his remarks. The *Wall Street Journal* quoted him endlessly. *Institutional Investor* had just named him the top-rated analyst on the Street. He knew everybody, and they knew him. His reports were beginning to drive stocks up, finally. That gave people hope.

Although Braun had been tainted, he was considered too smart, too relentless, too connected to be cast aside—a '90s Milken whom people couldn't help but gravitate toward, regardless of past sins. Other analysts liked having Braun back in the saddle. He lent a certain gravitas to a market trying to right itself. Investors liked him because he was beginning to make money for them again. CNBC liked him because he gave them pithy quotes and

13

reminded them of the good old days. His appearances were beginning to boost their ratings. People were in a forgiving mood.

Even the Sartos, who ran the diner back in Michigan, had made contact again. His recommendations in the late 90s had lost them $20,000 of their hard-earned money. Guilt prompted him to cover them out of his own pocket. They went their separate ways, but only a month ago they had sent him a letter saying they saw an interview with him, had decided to invest in a couple of companies based on his comments and had made some money.

The CEOs of the tech companies who hadn't given up liked him because he stroked their egos and re-validated their visions. They, in turn, were beginning to throw their investment banking business to Teestone, albeit within the confines of the newly reinforced, so-called Chinese walls that were supposed to exist between the investment banking and analyst sides of the house.

It was Braun's Man-in-the-Arena tenacity that had won over Aaron Cannondale. Aaron kept a copy of Teddy Roosevelt's words in his pocket: "… the man who is actually in the arena; whose face is marred by the dust and sweat and blood; who strives valiantly; who errs and comes short again and again; who knows the great enthusiasms, the great devotions and spends himself in a worthy cause …"

Aaron had run across Braun back in the day. How had a former ski mask and beauty aid outfit transformed itself into a telecom company? Braun. How had a former wholesale fish company converted itself into a wireless player? Braun. The way Aaron saw it, he needed a guy like Braun to help him give flight to what he had in mind. So it wasn't completely surprising that while Braun was standing there in line for a grilled cheese sandwich and a chocolate milk at Rebecca's, his cell phone rang. He stepped out of line and made his way down one of the small aisles for more privacy.

"Braun speaking."

"It's Vaughn." Terry Vaughn: the investment banking guru at Teestone, Friend of Cannondale, and arguably one of the most connected guys on the Street. "Jack, did you catch Cannondale's speech at the UN this week?"

"Cannondale? He's been out of the news for a while."

"We all have."

Braun grinned a knowing grin. "I didn't hear the speech, no. What did he have to say?"

"Same old digital divide crap. He called me the other day, Jack."

"And? He's not getting into fiber optics, is he? It would be a bit late to go down that path."

"Not exactly. But he's onto something."

"Like what?"

"He's not saying, entirely. I get the impression that he's looking around."

"Interesting."

"It is. I know I don't need to tell you this, Jack, but he's one of the elephants."

"I know."

"We lose him, and … well … you can kiss more than just bonuses goodbye this year."

"I understand, Terry."

"It's important to keep guys like him happy. Lord knows we could use the juice. The last couple of years haven't exactly …"

"Terry, I get it."

"I know you do. Come by on Thursday and I'll fill you in on what I know."

"Done."

"Oh, and Jack."

"Yeah, Vaughn."

"That buy rating you put on Western Line."

"Yeah."

"Nice. They were very pleased."

"They should be. It was a gift."

"Talk to you, Jack."

Chapter 3

"Monique, Graham here. Listen, I'm on my mobile so I might lose you. Tell Alfred that I need that dossier finalized in a fortnight … What's that? … Madrid? … Fine … but I need to get back to Brussels the following day … Who? Tell them it'll have to wait until after my speech … Listen, I'm about to walk into the conference hall. I'll have to call you back …"

Sir Graham Eatwell stood taller than he had at any time during his career. He was in Paris for a technology conference. The big guns of the day were there: the former head of Vivendi, senior executives from Hewlett-Packard, Intel and IBM. France's minister of technology was present, as were his German and Dutch counterparts.

As European Commissioner for Competition, Eatwell was one of the most powerful men in Europe. He could play God by deciding which mergers and acquisitions could go through—not just European companies, but global companies. He could also bust up cartels and throw his weight around when it came to providing aid to EU member countries.

In the three years since Eatwell had joined the Commission, he had successfully grabbed turf from other commissioners in an effort to transform the role of Competition Tsar into something with incisors. By all accounts, he had been successful. The rest of the world didn't get the European Union. That much was clear. It didn't understand what went on in the paneled backrooms there. A Brussels-watcher once said of the European Commission that "if it had a sense of theater to match its mission, its members would gather for their meetings in a dimly lit medieval hall, clad Jedi-style in flowing robes, and accompanied by a lightsaber-wielding palace guard."

This was all fine to Eatwell. He kind of liked it that way. The world may not understand Europe, but it sure as hell was going to respect it, at least on his watch.

He rose to the podium with characteristic poise. He liked the way his suit fell on his body. Cameras flashed. The conference host introduced him in French. He shook the gentleman's hand, took off his watch, and placed it on the side of his speech book to time himself. People clapped. He was popular. Few things were quite as gratifying as being the center of attention:

"*Mesdames et messieurs*," Eatwell said without an accent. "*Merci pour m'avoir donné aujourd'hui cette opportunité. The* economic state of Europe is sound."

(Applause)

"The headlines of late depict a bruised Europe, a stumbling Europe.

We are experiencing a period of introspection about who we are and what it means to be European. The people of Europe are speaking, and the obedient bureaucrats of Brussels must listen.

But I hope our period of introspection is brief. I hope that as we emerge from our torpor, we gain strength from the array of successes that our European Union has wrought.

Europe has a single currency in its pocket for the first time since the florin or possibly even the denarius. We have expanded our membership to 27 countries. But we have not lost sight of the ideals that brave men like Monnet and Schumann put forward after the Second World War."

(Applause)

"We should take pride in what we have accomplished. But we cannot rest.

A new century is upon us—a century that will be driven, perhaps like no previous century—by technology and innovation."

(Applause)

"We have proven to the world that by working together we can prevent war and bloodshed.

We are a model for economic cooperation. We are a leader.

You see it in our labs, in our companies, and in the marketplace.

Mark my words, a day will come in the not too distant future when Europe will have its own Microsoft … or Google."

(Applause)

Eatwell could feel the energy rising from somewhere within him.

He was born to talk like this. He was tailor-made to stir

a crowd.

"… Take Europe's global satellite positioning system, Galileo.

Until now, we have been dependent on the GPS infrastructure that the American military put in place.

And we have benefited. But soon, we will have a fully-functioning system of our own—a European system, built by Europeans for Europeans."

(Applause)

Eatwell paused for effect. He was at a point in his career where he could say what he meant, not what he felt he had to say. He was laying it on the line—take it or leave it. He took the audience through a quick review of the EU's technology budget. He pointed to areas of progress in various member states. He riffed a bit on how the Mediterranean was the cradle of Western civilization, and how it once again was poised to teach the world.

At the twenty-minute mark, the watch that he had placed on the podium made a low-pitched beep. He always tried to keep his speeches to 20 minutes. Anything more was gratuitous; anything less, incomplete.

"These are important gatherings.

But as we gather, let us keep one thing in mind.

We are a privileged people—privileged by the wear and tear of time to know our strengths and weaknesses.

And when it comes to technology, we are far from weak. We are strong. We have choices.

We can treat this conference as just another

conference, or we can treat it as the start of something.

For our collective sake, I hope we choose the latter. Thank you."

The crowd clapped. Several members of the audience stood, followed by more, and still more until the majority of the room was on its feet. Eatwell had connected. He had shamed them and then played the pride card. It always worked.

Chapter 4

More than 640 kilometers away in the small Dutch university town of Groningen, a twenty-nine-year-old graduate student named Peter Van Weert watched Eatwell's speech on TV. The hair on the back of his neck stood on end. Peter didn't like Eatwell, or his toff accent, but this Eurocrat had spoken the truth. Europe needed to get off its ass. Peter had tired of reading about young Americans his age with half his talent who had managed to cash in their dot.com millions before things had gotten really ugly. Deep down, he knew the tech revolution would bounce back, and when it did, he wanted a piece of it—he wanted the buckets of money, the notoriety, and the respect. His problem was that he was lazy. He didn't like to work all that hard. And he preferred to let his ideas speak for themselves.

Most of his ideas eddied around the subject of water. More than hash, more than sex, more than John Wayne westerns, Peter was consumed with water. It had always been a big deal to him. Growing up in the northern part of the Netherlands, it could not be avoided. When the warm winds of spring prevailed, his family would sail the choppy waters between Holland and Denmark. At other times they would visit friends in Hoorn, where they would rent a flat-bottomed Friesian boat for three or four days, wandering the calm waves of the IJsselmeer, formerly the South Sea until a series of storms and floods forced the Dutch to build a 19-mile long dike that turned it into a fresh water lake.

"I never really left the placenta," Peter used to say in his undergrad days when he was feeling intoxicated by the power of H2O. His pals thought he was a bit odd. He couldn't believe that a decade had gone by since then, but it had. The millennium had come and gone. He was now in year seven of his PhD. He had decided once and for all that it would be his final year. What he would do next, he hadn't a clue, but he was somewhat confident that it would be related to an idea that had been swishing around in his head for some time. The Eurocrat's speech brought it to the fore once again.

Peter walked over to his stereo, turned on some Brahms and fired up his computer. He was restless. He had wanted to get away for a while and started surfing the Web for cheap airfares to Rome. The Internet connection was painfully slow. After minutes of waiting for a page to load, Peter smacked his fist on the table, knocking over a glass of water. The water oozed across the uneven contour of the wooden desktop, rolling toward the lowest part of the plain. Hanging on a cork board on the wall just above the place where the water dripped off the table, hung a postcard of New York—an old one dated by the presence of the World Trade Center towers sticking out their chests.

"*Grote ver Jezus* (Jesus Christ)," he whispered to himself.

With that, Peter threw himself into a week of monastic isolation. No phone calls, no nightcaps at the bar, no football. He stocked up on cheese and plunged into a fit of research that at times felt dreamlike. What emerged was an esoteric description of how the world's water supply could be used to transmit voice, video, and data to homes and offices through the municipal water network. It was a big idea. For Peter, it was up there with Newton's apple. He wrote it all down, put it in an envelope, dropped it in his tutor's mailbox on an uncharacteristically sunny Friday afternoon, and headed to the graduate lounge for half-priced pints of Oranjeboom beer.

Chapter 5

Tuesday morning. A soccer ball phone blared next to Peter's head.

"Peter, can you come to my office this afternoon?"

"Why?"

"Your paper. We need to talk. I want you to meet somebody."

The door of his tutor's office had that kind of opaque, private investigator glass prevalent in Dashiell Hammett flicks. Peter knocked and went in.

"Ah, Peter, thanks for coming by. I want you to meet Phillipe Timmermans."

"Pleasure," Peter said.

"Timmermans is an old friend. We did our national service together in Belgium. Many years ago it seems now, huh, Phillipe?"

"It does, Alexi."

Trust wasn't a reaction that Timmermans immediately inspired in Peter. The man was thin and unusually tan for a Belgian. For someone in his early 50s, Timmermans lacked a single gray hair among a sea of black.

Probably dyed, Peter thought. Timmerman's eyes weren't exactly shifty, but they didn't seem to focus on any one thing for very long. The guy had confidence, though. Peter could feel it.

"Peter, I happened to be having dinner with Phillipe on Saturday evening. I mentioned your paper. Quite interesting, your idea."

"You showed it to him?" Peter said, annoyed.

"Relax, Peter. That's why I've asked you to come here. I'd like you to explain it to Phillipe yourself, that is, if you're comfortable doing that. What you're proposing doesn't belong in academia. It's too important, and it comes at a time when the technology universe could use a shot in the arm. Phillipe is an entrepreneur. He's done well for himself in diamonds, construction, and telecommunications."

"You did well in telecom?" Peter asked, incredulous.

"For a while," Timmermans said, smiling.

Peter scanned the room. His tutor could tell that he was a bit put out.

"Peter, you remember the time that you spent in Belgium? Remember how dismal the phone system was there? Remember how long it used to take to simply get a phone hooked up by the local company?"

"Yeah, months."

"Well, it now takes a day, partly because of the role this man played, and his contacts with the American phone company that bought a 51% stake in the Belgian company."

"Okay, so?"

"So I'd like to hear a bit more about your thoughts on water," Timmermans said, taking a silver cigarette case from the pocket of his yellow tweed jacket. "Of course, it's entirely up to you what you'd like to do with your idea, and frankly, I didn't understand most of what Alexi here was babbling about over dinner, but I sensed something bold and wanted to talk to you."

Peter looked straight through Timmermans as if he was somehow trying to assess his soul. After all, 30 minutes ago Peter had been under the duvet dreaming of scoring the winning corner kick for FC Groningen against Utrecht. Now a total stranger, the looks of whom he didn't even like, was being thrust upon him by a mentor whom he respected but who hadn't come to him first.

"I'm not sure about this," Peter said.

"Understandably," Timmermans said. "You don't know anything about me."

"Exactly."

"You're asking yourself, 'Who the hell is this guy?'"

"Right again."

"You'd prefer to get to know me."

"You were closer the first time."

Timmermans smiled and took a long drag from his Dunhill Blue.

"How about tonight?"

"What, tonight?"

"Dinner, on me. We can talk."

"Won't work. There's a match. FC Groningen."

"That's too bad. Unfortunately, I leave tomorrow for several days of business in Amsterdam," Timmermans said.

"Aren't you supposed to be in Amsterdam this week for a lecture?" Peter's tutor chimed in. Peter stared at him, clearly disturbed by the mention.

"I tell you what," Timmermans said, reaching for something in his sport coat. "No pressure. Let me leave you my card. We can arrange to meet the next time you are in Amsterdam. If you care to join me for dinner, the invitation stands."

Timmermans wrote out the name and address of a restaurant on the back of his business card, flipped it back over and handed it to Peter.

Chapter 6

Several weeks had come and gone since the meeting with Timmermans. It wasn't so much out of spite that Peter had procrastinated, more out of unease. Who the hell was this guy? Just another schlep desperately trying to get back in the tech game off someone else's idea—this time, his idea?

When Timmermans called Peter's tutor to say that Peter had been a no-show, the tutor paid Peter a visit. He said he understood Peter's reluctance and then got into the "you've been working on your PhD for seven years now" speech. Peter had heard it before, but the tutor was more persuasive this time. Peter *did* want to leave. He did want to see what it was like on the outside. He agreed to meet with Timmermans, but wouldn't guarantee when.

The air was crisp when Peter arrived at the Amsterdam train station. He bought a Coke, threw his bag over his shoulder, and walked outside to the rack of white municipal bikes that the government provided to the city's inhabitants free of charge. It was a clever way to deal with theft—give people free bikes that they can leave anywhere in the city, and they won't have to steal.

"Kapitein Zeppos" was the name of the restaurant that Timmermans had written on the back of the business card. Peter knew the place. It had taken its name from a '60s Belgian TV series, but that's not what Peter was thinking about as he pedaled. He was thinking of a youth hostel nearby. He had stayed there after a particularly drunken evening with buddies in the red light district. A bet had been put on the table that night which could not be resisted. One of his friends who was trying to stop smoking brazenly challenged the others that if he could go two days without a cigarette they would each have to eat 13 raw herring sandwiches with mayonnaise and pickles at the market in the morning. If willpower did not prevail and the friend did have a smoke, Peter and the others were to have the privilege of picking out the fattest, most exotic girl dancing in one of the windows along the *Oudezijds Achterburgwal* to service their mate. Raw herring won. It had to.

The rich smell of rijsttafel loitered outside an Indonesian restaurant as Peter turned a corner. He was still vacillating between meeting Timmermans or bailing. It was pretty clear what the Belgian wanted. Profit is the only motive of the businessman species. *But this idea, it was all just a harebrained notion scribbled on some paper. Didn't Timmermans realize that?* As much as Peter liked the idea, as much as he wanted to see it work, even he had his doubts about its viability.

Peter liked gliding through the narrow streets on the bike. There was an edge to Amsterdam that he appreciated. When Peter got to Zeppos, he parked the bike and had a quick smoke. From the street he could hear nothing, but suddenly someone opened a door, and a flood of laughter, glasses, music and Bohemia spilled out onto the cobblestones. It was his sort of place. Peter looked at his watch, checked the alley for Timmermans, stamped out his cigarette, and stepped over the threshold into this pleasant world.

A jazz trio played Brubeck's "Take Five." No sign of Timmermans. Peter ordered a beer and scanned the room. A couple made eyes at each other in the corner next to him. He hated that. A table of plump Eastern European businessmen toasted each other with vodka and howled at something funny. A man in his late 40s ate alone, pheasant with raisins and Sauerkraut.

Everything was normal, but something seemed odd. Then he spotted it. The drummer had one leg, the bass player was missing an ear, and the trumpet player had one hand.

"Peter, I'm glad you made it," Timmermans said, walking up from behind, coat off, as if he'd been there a while. "May I join you?"

"Of course. Cool place," Peter said, making stupid conversation. "I thought you'd like it."

Again, Timmermans pulled the silver cigarette case out of his jacket. It was clearly one of the Belgian's props. "So, let us talk about this technology of yours."

"You don't waste any time, do you?"

"Why should I? It's clear why we're both here."

"Is it?"

"Well, it's clear to me. Why are you here?"

"I heard good things about the band."

"I see. Why don't you tell me a bit more about your idea."

"You seem to already know a lot about it."

"Very little, actually. Your tutor didn't break too many confidences. I did try to pry it out of him, but he wouldn't budge."

"I don't even know you."

"I thought we had established that back in Alexi's office?"

"I know nothing of your business talent."

"True, although I can assure you it is excellent."

"I don't even know your taste in women, and that explains a lot about a man."

"True, as well, but once again, I can assure you that my taste is exceptional, and my senses are keen. That woman over there with that man, for example."

"Which one?"

"That one, there. She's a *fortuinzoeker* (gold digger)."

"You know this, how?"

"She laughs at everything that ugly bastard is saying. I'm guessing she grew up near Alkmaar. When she was young, she worked for her father—a cheese man. When he died, it was odd jobs—cleaning houses, working at the fish market, that sort of thing. She never went to college. Her first sexual encounter was at 16 with the older brother of the boy across the street. It was enjoyable enough that she tried it with other boys. She soon discovered the power that sex had over men—a power that, at first, was difficult for her to harness, a power that she was surprised a girl like her was capable of possessing. But it was tangible and good."

Peter was impressed by the assessment. "Close," he said. "But she's not from Alkmaar. I'd say she's from Hoorn. I used to spend summers there with my parents. Her accent is familiar. Her father was a fisherman."

"Very well. He was a fisherman then."

"Anyway, what's your story?"

A waitress appeared. "*Alstublieft.*"

"Glass of Pinot Grigio," Timmermans said.

"Beer," said Peter.

"Well, Peter, I was born in Mechelen and raised in Antwerp. I studied medieval philosophy at Leuven, couldn't feed myself, went to work in the construction business, made a lot of money, got married, got divorced ... got married again. It goes on from there. You?"

Peter looked surprised. He thought he was doing the interviewing. "My priorities are pretty simple. I would rank them as follows…"

"Let me guess," Timmermans said, scrunching his eyes and taking a drag of his Dunhill.

"Knock yourself out."

"I think your priorities would go something like: water, beer, football … women."

"Damn close," Peter said. "You forgot one."

Timmermans nodded as if to say, "Go ahead then."

"A 1974 Honda CR125M Elsinore motorcycle," Peter said proudly.

"Of course. Now really. Let's hear it—what's your story?"

"Born near Assen, still at Groningen University. Never want to get married. Hate liars. Have been studying water for a long time."

"What is it that fascinates you about water?"

"The fact that it's taken for granted."

The waitress returned with drinks. "*Alstublieft*."

"*Bedankt*. Can I trouble you for a glass of water?" Timmermans said.

Peter smiled at the irony. The Belgian actually had a sense of humor. "Why do you like business?" Peter asked, sipping his beer.

"It, too, is taken for granted. Everything has a buyer and a seller. When we're young, we bargain for approval. When we're seventeen, we bargain with girls to see which one will take her clothes off. When we go to the market, we haggle for the tastiest piece of meat. When we marry, we do so with the knowledge that no one woman can fulfill our deepest needs. It's a tradeoff between the 50,000 women out there you could choose from, and the one that comes into your life to whom you say 'yes,' or who says 'yes' to you. Sad thing is, most people don't want to make choices. They stroll through life listening to the hymn of comfort—too afraid or too settled to abandon what they have for the risk of something more meaningful, more right."

"Is that directed toward me?"

"Not unless it describes you. Does it?"

"What's considered right?"

"For me, it's having a feeling in your gut that is so right it hurts."

"Is that how you feel about my idea?"

"Absolutely. I think you ... we ... could make a lot of money."

"How?"

"I can't help but think that money must have been somewhere in the back of your mind when you wrote your paper. Can you not see it?"

"Not really."

"The world craved bandwidth before the dot.com meltdown, and it craves it now. It's like cocaine. Everyone is desperately trying to cram all those music CDs, Tom Cruise films, and endless lines of blogging through a pipe the size of a garden hose when what is needed is a fire hose at least."

Peter nodded.

"What you're proposing, Peter, if it works, is extraordinary, revolutionary. It was so obvious that no one saw it. My feeble brain isn't smart enough to understand how someone can send an email through the municipal water supply, but I can smell a good idea when it's put before me. I'm here because you've got the science and I have the contacts."

"What kind of contacts?"

"Businessmen, bankers, the kind of people who say 'I'll send the car to get you.'"

A waitress brushed Timmermans's back while balancing a plate of fish and potatoes with a warm buttery sauce.

Peter quietly played with his glass. "Maybe it's just a silly idea," Peter said.

"Doubtful," Timmermans said, unflinching. "Maybe I'm wrong."

"I don't think so."

"Maybe I'm already working with another venture capital guy."

"What's his name? I probably know him. If he's Dutch, good luck. You need American money, and even that's hard to come by these days."

"Maybe I just want to put my paper in my desk drawer."

"That would be stupid. That's what I'm trying to talk you out of. I knew guys like you in Leuven. Permanent students. Smart guys. They're now world-class connoisseurs of late-night kebabs, beer, and 21-year-old language students. I want to save you from that, Peter."

"What's wrong with 21-year-old language students?"

"Listen, your idea is good, Peter. You owe it to the world not to keep this in your head."

"I don't owe anybody, anything, thank you very much."

"Look. It's as simple as this. Let me help you make a lot of money," Timmermans said, staring deeply into Peter's eyes as if he was trying to hypnotize him.

"And help yourself," Peter said.

"And help myself. You're 29 years old. Imagine retiring at 31. Imagine that. What would you do?"

Peter thought for a moment. "I don't know."

"Come on. You must have an idea."

"Move to Wyoming, I suppose. Buy a lot of guns. Date women with big hair. I think I'd like it out there."

"I can get you there, Peter."

"How?"

"Patent the technology, form a company, bring in some gray hairs like myself to run the place."

"You can make that happen?"

"Yes."

Peter paused. The trio finished its set and made its way to the bar. The Eastern Europeans shoveled food into their mouths. Two women kissed. The scene felt right. They were his kind of people in his kind of place. But he suddenly felt overcome with a desire to say his good-byes, as if he were going on a trip. He visualized Kapitein Zeppos twenty years down the road. He saw the same group of people eating, enjoying themselves, but not laughing as deeply. He saw older visages on the wounded jazz trio, and the same plate of fish and potatoes being served to the table next to him. Same waitress, same smell, same music. He remembered an ad for a dude ranch that he had cut out from the back of a magazine...

"*There's a place in the Wyoming mountains where time slows down, the air smells clean, the water runs pure,*"

and the people are down-home friendly. Boulder Lake Lodge is truly at the 'end of the road,' nestled in the foothills of the Bridger National Forest. Thick aspen groves and pine-covered hillsides set the stage for one of the finest vacations in the Wind River Mountains."

Timmermans smoked his Dunhill.

Peter didn't like this Belgian, but he was beginning to sense the man was for real. Peter began to speak, stopped himself, and then started again. "What would we call it?"

"What?" Timmermans said.

"The company. What would we call it?"

Timmermans paused for a moment to take a deep hit on the cigarette. "Whatever you want, Peter," he said, smoke slinking out his nose.

"Cheyenne."

Timmermans looked confused. "What's that?"

"Capital of Wyoming."

Chapter 7

Aaron had read somewhere that the first mention of the Château de La Rochepot in Burgundy was in the 13th century. Once upon a time, it was probably used as a Gallo-Roman defense. Partially wrecked during the French Revolution it was later restored beginning in 1893 when it was bought by Mme Cecile Sadi Carnot, wife of the then-President of France, Marie François Sadi Carnot.

But that's not what Aaron Cannondale liked about the Château de La Rochepot. He liked it because it had a drawbridge and a watch wall and a Chinese room—all the things that reminded him of boyhood fantasies—battling forces of evil, crossing the water, storming the walls, saving the damsel in distress. He liked it because he could have it, or a version of it. He also had houses in Martha's Vineyard, Osaka, and Bermuda.

It took several hundred laborers four years to build Aaron's replica of the Château de La Rochepot high in the Wasatch Mountains above Salt Lake City. He called it "Kshanti" or "patience," one of the six Buddhist paramitas that makes us one with who we truly are. Two workers had died during the construction, and Aaron had gotten badly beaten up in the press.

"Who doesn't underpay laborers?" Aaron erupted in an aside as he dictated notes for an upcoming speech to Hayden in the chateau's "China Room."

"These guys want to work," Aaron said. "It's the American way - 'Give me your tired your poor, your huddled masses yearning to breathe free, the wretched refuse of your teeming shore. Send these, the homeless, tempest-tossed to me: I lift my lamp beside the golden door…' One group comes over en masse and works its collective butt off. Then another group comes over. The latecomers earn less than those who came before them. It's the price of admission, for God's sake," Aaron said, pacing back and forth with a bottle of lemon-flavored Perrier in his hand.

"Let's be clear about something, Aaron. I'm not quoting Emma Lazarus in this speech."

"Why not?"

"Because it's cheese, that's why. They will laugh at you."

"So patriotism is dead. Is that it, old boy?"

"I'm not saying that."

"What are you saying?"

"I'm saying patriotism has its time and place. It has to be pulled out sparingly. Otherwise, it'll get as watered down as Christmas and become one more sacred thing lost to the Madison Avenue crowd."

"My, aren't we a sensitive soul. Fine, Hayden. You win. We'll go light on the patriotism. Hayden, let me ask you something."

"Sure."

"Are you going to write a kiss and tell about this when it's all over?"

The question took Hayden off guard. It was a

particularly prescient question considering that after only a few months on the job Aaron had asked Hayden if he would help him write a book. It was unclear what kind of book it would be, or what title they would give it, or even what the book would be about, but Aaron felt he was working on something big, and he wanted it chronicled. Having agreed to work with Aaron on the book, Hayden found himself regularly scribbling in a small notepad or dictating voice notes into a handheld micro-recorder.

"No, Aaron. Kiss and tells aren't my style. I'm going to write the book that you say you want to write, the one that's causing me to follow you around like a Labrador."

Aaron smiled a knowing smile. "Good man, good man."

Aaron's cell phone rang. He looked at the incoming number. "Gotta take this one. Back in a second," he said with a wink.

Aaron walked out of the room. Hayden couldn't remember ever seeing Aaron in anything other than a suit—expensive suits. He almost exclusively wore Armani or Cerruti. Hayden wondered what it would be like if the tables were turned, if he were the rich guy and Aaron was the wordsmith. Why not? Not too long ago, Hayden had seriously thought about starting a dot.com. Who hadn't? He had written the business plan, and sweet talked a couple of friends who were working at banks on Wall Street, but in the end, it didn't feel right.

It wasn't that he didn't have salesmanship in his blood.

His family came from a long line of low-country entrepreneurs on his mother's side. Sure, he could sell when he needed to, but he couldn't imagine doing it on a daily basis, and that's what it took to be someone like Aaron. You had to get off on "the deal." You had to relish haggling. You had to be the most vocal sonofabitch at the bazaar. Most of all, you had to consistently care about these sorts of things, and Hayden just didn't care that much about these things, at least not consistently.

Hayden could understand how deal making could become addictive, but it wasn't the kind of juice that got him going. What got Hayden going were words. That was the road he had chosen. And not just any kind of road, either. He didn't have much patience for the meandering country paths of the navel-gazing romantics. And although they had their place, he didn't have much stomach for the angst-ridden curves inherent in the exhaustive social commentary he found with some writers. No, what Hayden liked were the straightaways—the long stretches of uncomplicated scenery that most people could agree upon.

He sensed that in Aaron he had finally found a client that felt the same way. Although for Aaron, leaning too heavily at all toward the examination of things was detrimental. Contemplative observation and empire building didn't mix. No, a guy like Aaron needed to focus on one thing and one thing only—business, no diversions.

At the end of the day, Hayden was confident that he and Aaron agreed on the basics. Maybe that was why he found it relatively easy to find Aaron's voice when writing for him. Though their backgrounds and ages were different, and though they had never traded notes on their biases, Hayden was pretty sure that they looked at the world through a similar prism. In a nutshell: government was a thing designed to help people improve themselves, not a maid service to clean up after everyone. Technology was a tool for mankind, not its savior. Mediterranean food was art. Life was to be attacked, not viewed on television. Americans needed more holidays. Brazilian women were hot. Russian women, on the whole, were not. Jazz was medicinal. The three best smells in the world in no particular order were rain, bacon, and Tiger Lilies. God was happy the day he created Italy because he lavished it with olive oil, garlic, anchovies, parmesan cheese, and cannolis.

Frank Sinatra had a great voice but was a punk. People should not eat while walking down the street or riding on the subway. People who don't listen or who use words such as "like" and "you know" must be destroyed. Confidence was not something to be ashamed of. New Year's Eve was not fun. Cigarettes should be good for you. Judaism, Islam, Christianity, and Buddhism were the world's varsity religions; everything else was JV. Capital punishment was a failure of human imagination. Airlines—all airlines—had an extra hot seat reserved for them in hell somewhere in the middle of a five-seat row next to a very large man with bad breath who liked to talk.

Yeah, he and Aaron had a lot in common, but somehow

he knew that Aaron wouldn't hesitate to cut him loose and kick him to the curb when he was done with him.

Aaron returned from the other room with a cat-ate-the-mouse look on his face.

"You look pleased about something," said Hayden.

"I am. Let's call it quits on the speech today. Can I show you something?"

"Sure."

They walked through several antechambers until they came to a high-ceilinged room decorated with black granite tables, halogen lights, and brushed steel. It was Aaron's media room. A wall of flat-screen TVs stood in the corner, 10 across, 10 high. None of them had the volume on. Screen one: rage in the streets of Gaza. Screen four: two teenage daredevils scurrying down a hilly San Francisco thoroughfare on street luges. Screen seven: a well-coiffed couple with cocaine smiles attempting to sell the public a fragile-looking rotisserie. Screen eight: a polyester-clad minister leading his congregation in bowed prayer, only *his* eyes are open. Screen ten: a lion mating with a lioness on an African plain. Screen three: a talk show host supervising a brawl between two clans from the same trailer park. Screen six: enormous man stirring a pot of spicy crawdads.

To the left of the TV wall was a large computer screen with several images broken up into grids. One of the images looked like a live shot of London.

"That's Trafalgar cam," Aaron said, smiling. He pointed to other images on the screen. "That there is the

Machu Picchu cam. And that ... that's my favorite ... K2 base camp cam." Aaron had installed his own private Internet cameras in these places, the planet's most beautiful sights at his fingertips.

"You're allowed to set up cameras on K2?" Hayden asked incredulously.

"*I* am."

Kshanti was one seriously wired place. A handful of graphics workstations were lined up along another wall.

"Those are for the boys," Aaron said. He always referred to the posse of software geniuses who worked for him as "the boys." Sometimes when he'd wake up in a sweat late at night with aspirations of changing the world, he'd summon them to crank out code over bottomless plates of toro and sushi rolls.

"Come in here," Aaron said, leading Hayden through a wood-paneled corridor with heraldic coats of arms, medieval broadswords, claymores, targes, axes, and dirks. Hayden called it Aaron's "Rob Roy" hallway.

They came to a grand room. One entire wall was made of glass. Through the glass, the splendor of the Wasatch spanned in front of them. Hayden had never seen a mountain panorama quite like it. A western sun-splashed into the room, casting shadows over the dark wood, peach-colored vases and viga ceiling. Navajo rugs lay strewn across the brick flooring. Coyote skulls hung on the walls. In the corner was a desk that looked like a pilot's cockpit. Parked in front of it was a single chair. Aaron sat down. It was one of his favorite toys—another remote-controlled console that allowed him to command things from a distance without having to see them or interact with them directly.

"Watch." With a flick of a switch, the glass facade began to open. The smell of wild sage and dry air flooded into the room. Aaron flicked other switches. On a series of TV monitors, Hayden could see hidden doors open, book shelves turn, lights go on and off, and paintings change within their frames.

"That's all very close to home," Aaron said boyishly. "But what about from afar?"

Aaron hit more buttons. On one of the TV monitors, Hayden could see the front of Aaron's home in Hamilton. Aaron tapped something. Suddenly, the lights within the Bermuda home turned on. Aaron tapped again; the lights went off. Another screen, another image, this time cattle far down in the valley beneath Kshanti. They began to herd and run off in the same direction.

"Audio herding," Aaron said, laughing. "I had them put speakers down there."

A satellite phone hung on the side of the console. Aaron picked it up, dialed, and pointed to an image on a monitor. It was his 10-acre place at Martha's Vineyard. Hayden had never been there, but he knew from conversations that it was as high-tech as Kshanti. Among the bells and whistles were a bowling alley, a virtual reality room, and one wing devoted entirely to paintballing.

Hayden had heard that Aaron had also installed vending machines in just about every room where you could order a drink from your cell phone. On the monitor was an image of a flag pole in front of the house with Old Glory waving in the sunlight. Aaron played with the console. The flag began to lower.

"Hayden, I'd like you to come to Brussels with me next week. Cancel whatever you've got. I need you on this one. That call I took, it was from a Belgian friend. Name is Timmermans. Smokes a lot. He has started a company. It's going to be big. He's looking for money. I intend to get in on the ground floor. Remember something, Hayden."

"What's that?"

"Wabi/sabi."

"Wasabi?"

"No, wabi/sabi? It's Zen. It means that the value of something comes from its imperfections. Timmermans is a good businessman, but I guarantee you that he won't be able to bring as much value to this new company as I can. Come with me. I want you to get some color for my book. I may also want to give an unannounced talk at the American Chamber of Commerce on this whole bandwidth issue. The Euros are hapless. Come with me, Hayden. It'll be fun."

"I don't know."

"Come on. Let me ask you something."

"Sure."

"You like to get inside the heads of the people you write for, right?"

"As much as I can."

"You want to get to know them, the soul inside the suit, that sort of thing, right? You want to know what gets them jazzed, what bores them, what scares them, who they hate, who they love, who they want to disembowel. Am I right?" Aaron seemed to have a sixth sense, an ability to relate to whomever he was talking to on that person's terms, regardless of the subject.

"That's exactly right," Hayden said, a bit spooked.

"Well, that's what I'm offering you, a chance to ride along—a front row seat on the Cannondale Express. What do you say?"

"Fine, Aaron, I'll go."

"Excellent."

Aaron returned to the screen with the flag at Martha's Vineyard. "Charlie," Aaron shouted into the satellite phone." I thought I asked you to lower the flag promptly at 5:00 p.m. every night? Well, you're 15 minutes late. I thought I'd help you out. Send someone out there to get it. And hey, check the vending machine in the living room. I just bought you a Coke."

God, Aaron's staff must hate that, Hayden thought. He watched as Aaron continued to play with his toys, controlling things from a distance.

Chapter 8

According to the International Association for the Properties of Water and Steam, the water molecule consists of two hydrogen atoms and one oxygen atom. The three atoms make an angle; the H-O-H angle is approximately 104.5 degrees. The center of each hydrogen atom is approximately 0.0957 nm from the center of the oxygen atom. This molecular structure leads to hydrogen bonding, which is a stabilized structure in which a hydrogen atom is in a line between the oxygen atom on its own molecule and the oxygen on another molecule.

The average human body is about 60% water. The brain is close to 80 percent water; plasma is about 90 percent water. Raindrops are not tear-shaped; they look more like small hamburger buns.

A black Mercedes sped through Brussels. Hayden sat next to Aaron in the back seat, looking out on the Flemish facades as Aaron spoke on his cell phone. The car turned onto Avenue Louise, one of the city's grander streets. Aaron hadn't told Hayden much about his friend Timmermans or about the company the Belgian was starting. What little information Hayden was able to glean came from Henry Neville—a small, strange man who acted as Aaron's personal research assistant. At least, that's the label that made the most sense to Hayden. Neville was bookish, in his 50s, and prided himself on mnemonic feats of intellectual strength—the ability to recite long Kipling poems, or to play several games of chess simultaneously while blindfolded, or to memorize batting averages for the entire American League. Hayden had heard these Neville stories from Aaron and dictated them into his micro-recorder for Aaron's book.

Neville was employed by Aaron primarily because Aaron had an annoying habit of questioning the facts of someone's story. He had no shame in putting the person on the spot, in front of others, in the middle of his dinner parties. He'd throw down the gauntlet, saying, "Are you sure about that?" or "I doubt that very much—going to have to get my man, Neville, on that." And with that, he'd scribble something on a napkin and have one of the wait staff take it down to Neville for analysis. At some point during the dinner, the staff would deliver a note to Aaron, who would impishly announce to the room, "By the way, Neville looked into that minor detail we were discussing earlier, and you were wrong."

Hayden liked this game of Aaron's. He was inclined to do the same thing when he found himself in a conversation with someone who was talking out of their cake hole, but he didn't have the luxury of having a Neville on the payroll. He imagined a Quasimodo-type figure locked up somewhere in the cellar of Kshanti, surrounded by walls of computers. Hayden had never actually laid eyes on Neville. They communicated by phone or email. One of the perks of being Aaron's speechwriter was access to Neville's services. Hayden regularly took him up on it.

Indeed, the day after Aaron had invited Hayden to

Brussels, Hayden sent an email to Neville asking for additional fodder on bandwidth issues. Neville's responses were normally curt, thorough, and humorless. Despite Hayden's many attempts to get the man to crack some sort of cyber smile through their emails, Neville wasn't interested. On this particular day, though, Neville was downright chatty. He told Hayden that it was uncanny that he was asking for information on bandwidth because Aaron had himself asked for information on the same subject, in addition to a background check on some Dutch graduate student and a lot of information on water. He volunteered that he hadn't seen Aaron do quite so much homework on a subject in a long time. He also mentioned that Aaron's lobbyist in Washington, Elliot Pettigrew, was bombarding him with requests on international merger and acquisition law. Neville complained to Hayden that all this research was taking valuable time away from his latest pursuit—memorizing Swiss train timetables.

Aaron powered off his cell phone. "Do you like truffles?" he asked, slapping Hayden's knee.

"Who doesn't?"

"I don't."

"Sorry to hear that."

"Not to worry. Listen, we're meeting some people at a place called La Trouffe Sympatique. Every course is served with truffles. I'd like to ask a favor. You speak French, right?"

"Yes."

"What about Dutch?"

"No."

"Alright then, let me give you the lay of the land. Timmermans will, of course, be there. In addition to French, he also speaks Dutch, or Flemish, you know what I mean. Don't be surprised if he slips into multiple tongues with his colleague during the meeting."

"Which colleague?"

"A young Dutch student named Peter Van Weert. He's the tech geek behind this company. We must make him feel part of this."

"What is 'this,' Aaron? I still don't get what's going down here exactly."

"Did you read the article?"

Before they left, Aaron had tossed Hayden a copy of a European money magazine. It contained a piece about Timmermans' new company, "Cheyenne," that had just been formed in the Netherlands. Despite Hayden's tech background, Cheyenne's goal seemed like fantasy. The premise was devilishly simple: provide virtually unlimited bandwidth to people's homes through the existing system of municipal water pipes.

At first, Hayden was a bit surprised that Aaron seemed to be jumping into the technology so quickly, but then again, Aaron was the sixth richest man in the world; he, Hayden, was not. It was Aaron's willingness to take such risks that had made him so rich. And the more Hayden thought about the technology, the more it actually made sense.

One of the great technology battles of the '90s that still raged into the first decade of the new century was the competition between telephone, satellite, Internet, cable, and electric power companies to control the "last mile" of service to individual homes and businesses. Own the last mile and you controlled customer access to telephone, TV, movies, music, and the Internet. Own the last mile and you made a lot of money.

Clearly, Aaron was contemplating an alternative to the last mile—water—and he didn't mind going all the way to the Netherlands to get it. Timmermans acted as Cheyenne's CEO. In the article that Hayden had read, Timmermans explained that Cheyenne's plan was to offer a device that connected the main water supply running into homes and businesses with people's computers. Digitized information sent from the computers would flow through the water pipes to the local water utility, which in turn would use Cheyenne-supplied technology to convert the signal and link customers up to the Internet. Data would bounce from utility to utility through water pipes across Europe, and eventually beyond. In areas that did not have adequate access to the Internet backbone, signals would have to be beamed up to satellites.

"Just tell me what Timmermans says if he slips into French for any reason, will you?" Aaron asked, smiling.

Clearly, Aaron didn't entirely trust his friend Timmermans. Maybe it was just "bizness," but it got Hayden thinking. He liked Aaron, liked him a lot. But he wasn't sure he trusted him. Of the little that Hayden knew about Aaron, he was aware that the man had been a software programmer early on. Beyond that, all he knew was that Aaron was an uncommon cocktail—one part geek to two parts Machiavelli. It's what took Lyrical from an "also ran" networking hardware company to one of the world's premier technology names.

Hayden had seen Aaron orchestrate deals where he successfully pitted techies and executives against each other without either side knowing. By the time it was all over, he had them handing out their sisters' phone numbers. Hayden was eager to witness the dance that was about to unfold.

"I mean to buy Cheyenne, Hayden," Aaron announced suddenly.

"Buy it?" Hayden almost shouted. "Why not just make an initial investment?"

"Oh, I'll do that. And then I'll buy it. Timmermans is getting too old to make this thing work. He needs me. He's going to screw it up. He doesn't want to see that happen. Neither do I. I don't like screw ups. No sir, I do not like screw ups, Hayden."

"Does Timmermans know that you intend to buy it?"

"He wants to sell."

"But does he know?"

"He knows."

"Anyone else?"

"Like who?"

"Like that kid, Peter?"

"No, Peter doesn't know."

"But Aaron, he's the brains behind the entire thing."

"Is he, Hayden? Is he really?" Aaron said with a penetrating look followed by a quick smile. And in that brief second, Hayden saw it—that "kill or be killed" instinct that Hayden imagined rose up in every species of animal around an African watering hole in the dead of summer when it's hotter than hell, and the water table is balancing just above bone dry.

"The hell with him, Hayden. Now listen, from now on, I want to elevate this whole idea of bandwidth in my speeches. Every talk that I give—Davos, CeBIT, AARP, I don't care. We need to hit this message like a piñata. Nobody has quite figured out how to provide unlimited bandwidth yet. It's a land grab, Hayden, I'm sure of it. And, oh yeah, I hope you're taking good notes on what we're about to embark on here."

"Notes?"

"For my book, I mean."

"Right. I've already filled part of a notebook. Have you thought of a title yet?"

"No, have you?"

"No."

"We'll get there, Hayden. Don't worry. That's down the road. All I care about is hitting this bandwidth message. It's gonna be big…"

Hayden let Aaron go off on his stream of

consciousness carpet ride. No doubt, unlimited bandwidth would be a good thing. Even with DSL and cable modems, the Internet could be a tortoise. Hayden had often thought that waiting for Web pages to load on dial-up was a bit like waiting for southerners to finish their sentences.

"It might as well be me, right, Hayden? I mean, plenty of people talk about it. What counts is doing it, owning it. I know how to *own* things, Hayden. And then this kid—this wonderful Dutch kid ..."

"Peter?"

"Yeah. This kid who doesn't get up much before noon, this kid who finds it right there in a glass of water perched on some titty magazine next to his desk. You've gotta love that."

Yeah, you do gotta love that, Hayden thought to himself as the car pulled up to the restaurant.

"Oh, by the way, Hayden, in addition to being my speechwriter, you're now Director of Communications."

"What?"

"Yeah. I like the sound of it, don't you?"

"Director of Communications of what?"

"I don't know; we'll see."

Chapter 9

Aaron got out of the car first. "Monsieur Cannondale, *bonsoir*," the owner beamed from the steps, reaching to shake Aaron's hand. He was a small, fat sycophant with a painted Peter Lorre smile—the kind of smile that small, fat sycophants perfect. Claude was his name.

"*Ça va*, Claude?" Aaron said without accent. Hayden grinned. Typical Aaron charm. He didn't speak a word of French, but he could give the impression that he did. Inside, sumptuous women, most of whom looked more Latin than northern European, took their coats and guided them to the private room decorated in Victor Horta art nouveau.

"Don't get too friendly with these girls," Aaron whispered to Hayden. "They'll break your heart."

Hayden was introduced to Timmermans and to the boy wonder, Peter. He also met Cheyenne's talented but quiet CFO, Michelle Vandermullen. Hayden caught himself staring at her, but not before she had caught him. She was lovely—blonde, blue eyes, red lips, and a cream cheese complexion. Two of Cheyenne's lawyers were also there, as was Aaron's attorney—a pug-nosed Italian from Brooklyn named Fiorello Bertolini.

A throng of niceties ensued—handshakes, pats on the back, fake smiles. When the guests settled in, Claude read the menu: wild mushroom tarte with truffles, seared fois gras, asperges à la flamande, and escargot for starters. Grilled squab with potato truffle confit and swedes, tripe `a l'Armagnac, giant ravioli stuffed with wild boar and pumpkin, and steak topped with truffles and duck fat. Aperitifs were passed around—Campari, Kir Royale, Vodka, Port. Water with lemon for Aaron.

"Gentlemen," Aaron said with a sudden tone of seriousness. With that, one word the meeting had begun. "Let's get right to it. Valuation. How is the world going to value Cheyenne? It's not going to be an easy story to tell the general public. To some, it may sound like science fiction, but then again that's what I like about it."

Peter, who had been looking at Aaron skeptically from the get-go, finally pinpointed what he didn't like about this Cannondale. He reminded him of the cocky American business students he had come across while he studied at the University of North Carolina for a year. God, he disliked them—their arrogance, their one-dimensional pursuit, their almost religious belief in the power of capitalism to heal mankind's ills.

"Look, it's very simple, Aaron said. "Before I move on investing in this ... if I move on this ... the first thing we need to talk about is valuation."

"What are you talking about?" Peter said abruptly. Aaron ignored Peter at first but then turned directly toward him.

"How much do you think this thing is going to ultimately be worth, my friend?"

"I don't know. Millions, I suppose," Peter said.

"Millions, really?" Aaron said, slightly annoyed at

Peter's naiveté. "How many ... Two million? Two hundred? A billion?

"A billion sounds good," Timmermans joked.

"You see my point. It's ultimately only worth what the market says it's worth. And the market will value it more favorably when it knows that someone with a track record that speaks for itself has invested—someone who is willing to assume the risk."

"This is bullshit," Peter squawked. One of Cheyenne's lawyers put his hand on Peter's forearm.

"But that's why you came to *me*, isn't it?" Aaron said. "I am that someone. And this someone is saying that this will be big. It could deliver the true promise of the Internet that everyone has been gagging for over the past decade. Forget about delivering videos to people's doors, or online universities, or auctioning off your uncle's baseball cards online. That's old school. What we have before us is something that could fundamentally alter the way we live, work, play and trade."

Aaron was good. Right about here, Hayden thought he might have heard a choir of angels and cherubs with trumpets heralding the arrival of a new day. The door to the room opened. A waiter came in with a trolley of amuse bouche and wine.

Peter stood up. "Let's get something straight, Cannondale. You're not going to run this company."

"No, I'm not, Peter, that's right," Aaron said coolly. *You're* going to run it, along with Timmermans and

Michelle. I'm just going to be an investor."

The others laughed. Hayden felt bad for Peter. The kid was just beginning to realize that he was the only one at the table who wasn't on board. No one had consulted him.

"Timmermans, what the hell is going on here?" Peter asked, irate. "It's the best thing for Cheyenne, Peter," Timmermans said.

"You'll be taken care of."

"Taken care of? The hell with being taken care of. I don't need to be taken care of."

"Yes, you do," Aaron said. "We all do."

"Cut the philosophy, Cannondale," Peter said, getting hotter. "Timmermans?"

"It's just business, Peter."

Just business, Hayden thought to himself. What a funny little phrase. He never really understood what it meant. It was a license for two or more parties to obtain what they needed, or wanted. It could also be a license to put one's morality on a shelf until such time that one needed it again. There was a lot that Hayden didn't understand about business—a lot that he didn't want to understand. But he couldn't help but be glued to the bullfight playing out before him. Aaron was toying with the kid like a matador with a red cape.

"You're about to give the whole goddamn thing away, Timmermans," Peter said, hurt.

The lawyer, Bertolini, opened his leather attaché case. "Taking into account significant regulatory hurdles, the necessary coordination with the European Commission, and the initial risk involved with an unproven technology, Mr. Cannondale's Lyrical, through its U.S. subsidiary, Cheyenne Acquisition Corp., is prepared to make an initial investment of $90 million, leading to the eventual purchase of Cheyenne B.V. of the Netherlands, which our bankers currently value at several hundred million dollars."

Hayden saw Peter's face cringe. The lawyer speak had started. Translation: Cannondale, through his company, Lyrical, would take an initial 30% stake in Cheyenne, and no doubt, one day soon would ultimately own it.

Hayden could tell that Peter's mind was racing. He was in a sort of trance. A cynical grin spread across the kid's face that said, "So this is what it feels like to be cut out." From this point on, the destiny of Cheyenne would be in someone else's hands, and it hadn't even really started yet. Hayden tried to put himself in Peter's shoes. Then, all of a sudden, Peter came alive, as if he suddenly remembered Bertolini's words.

"How much did you say?" Peter blurted.

"Several hundred million," Bertolini said, pausing briefly in his legal recitation. Cheyenne's lawyers talked among themselves. Fingers wagged in the air.

Several hundred million. Damn, Hayden thought to himself as he looked over at Peter.

Chapter 10

Graham Eatwell had what he always had for dinner when he was feeling good about his ability to navigate the world—steak béarnaise, frites, a simple green salad dripping in vinaigrette, and a Côte de Beaune.

He had heard whisperings that Cannondale was in Brussels and that he had eaten at La Truffe Sympatique. Claude, the owner, was a good friend of Eatwell's. One phone call was all it took to get some clues as to what the dinner was about. In addition, Eatwell had a member of his staff track down details on Cheyenne.

This Yank, Cannondale, clearly had his sights set on grabbing Cheyenne—a *Dutch* company, a *European* company, after all—for himself. And if Eatwell let it happen, a golden nugget of technology born in Europe would be lost to the Americans. Once upon a time, the winds of technological advancement had blown from East to West from Prague, Budapest, Florence, Heidelberg, and Antwerp to the New World. But those winds had changed direction some time ago, and that ate at Eatwell. The things they talked about in Silicon Valley—things he didn't entirely understand—were now exported the other way, to the Grandes Places of Europe.

Cannondale had taken his 30% investment in Cheyenne. Soon, he would, no doubt, make his play for the whole company, and Eatwell would be forced to make a decision. It wouldn't be easy saying no to Cannondale, but that's exactly what Eatwell intended to do. He didn't even need to look at the facts. In this situation, facts were irrelevant.

Eatwell's speech in Paris had achieved the desired effect, which was to whip up the European business community into a frenzy to make them feel proud of their creative heritage, and then shame them for having accepted their fate as technological "also-rans" to the Americans. The head of the European Commission had decided that the European Union was going to take growth and innovation seriously, and Eatwell was going to see that they made good on that. Eatwell wanted to reinforce the fact that the winds of technological change could once again be reversed.

Bernard, Eatwell's butler, served more wine as Eatwell watched a woman through his dining room window. She was letting her black Bouvier relieve itself against a horse-chestnut tree out on Avenue Tervuren. Brussels could be dreary, but it was Eatwell's home now. It had been for a while. He had come a long way from the stone walls of an English boarding school. If there was one thing he had taken with him from those days, it was the concept of self-preservation. That lesson had come early, among the fresh faces of the next generation of the entitled. Boys became men and went on to run banks and companies and law firms and rarely spoke of that day when they were introduced to that enduring public school tradition of being bent over and used as toast racks by bullying seniors.

Come to think of it, the concept of self-preservation went back even further for Eatwell, to the days before boarding school, during the war, when, as young boys, Eatwell and his friend Menno Kuipers were scooped up by their parents and moved to Bletchley Park.

It was a lonely place, Bletchley, especially for a kid. The adults would disappear for hours at a time to solve their mathematical riddles in rooms where children were not invited. Eatwell and Kuipers didn't actually mind. It gave them more time to play. But somehow they knew, even at that young age, that they had all been on the side of unquestionable good. It was so binary—good vs. evil, very little grey. What was done to defeat fascism had to be done and the hell with the nasty little compromises. The world had depended on people like their parents. Eatwell and Kuipers had grown up, and now the world depended on men like them.

Eatwell was a heavyweight in Brussels, and Kuipers had become the Minister of Transport and Waterworks in the Netherlands. Waterworks dealt with the more technical aspects of the country's complex system of dikes and canals. It was a seemingly mundane corner of the Dutch bureaucracy, but the dossier was broad and powerful. It branched out to technology, transportation, trade, and international law of the sea. Cheyenne's technology would, no doubt, fall under Kuipers' umbrella, and that made Graham very happy indeed.

How fantastically strange life is, Eatwell thought to

himself—to think that he and Kuipers would again be on the same side of good as they had been when they were young boys. *How utterly sublime* it was that he and his old Bletchley playmate would again have the opportunity to defeat a common foe, in this case, Cannondale, whom he would take particular pleasure in taking down.

Tomorrow, Eatwell would ring Kuipers. He wanted his friend to be prepared. More important, he wanted to hear the resolve in Kuipers' voice—a resolve that both of them would need in order to stand up to Cannondale. Eatwell wanted to know that Kuipers still felt as strongly as he did about this experiment called the European Union.

"Your dinner, sir," Bernard announced.

"Thank you, Bernard."

"Shall I pour?"

"Yes. And pour a glass for yourself."

"Sir?"

"Join me, Bernard. Eating alone is so dismal."

Bernard poured the wine, wiped his hands on his apron, and drew the chair at the far end of the long table from Eatwell. They chatted. The meat was good with the creamy béarnaise. It was all good, save the loneliness.

They had all left his life, one by one—his parents, his colleagues at Downing Street. All had gone on to fame or faded obscurity. He was okay with it, though. He had found that life was a bit that way, a series of decks on a cruise ship. Some decks were music and laughter and drink. Some were reserved for pondering. Still others, like the captain's bridge, kept the vessel on course. That's where Eatwell saw himself firmly perched at this moment in time, at the helm. Yes, Europe needed him to make the right decisions, however unpopular. He would not shun his responsibilities in carrying this vessel called the European Union to port. Problem was, he wasn't entirely certain where that port was.

"Bernard, what say you of the Canary Islands this time of year?" Eatwell said, making himself a perfect mouthful of steak, a couple of frites, salad, and a daub of béarnaise at the end of his fork.

"Good weather right about now, I imagine, sir."

It was going to be all right. Eatwell would see to it.

Part II
Chapter 11
(2005)

Cheyenne was humming. Timmermans and his CFO, Michelle, had taken it public in the Netherlands. It was now trading as an American Depository Receipt (ADR) on the NASDAQ in New York, which allowed Americans to purchase shares. The company didn't have customers yet, but the stock had almost doubled on the promise of riches alone.

Timmermans was spending almost all of his time negotiating endless partnership agreements between Cheyenne and municipal water suppliers throughout Europe to allow communications signals to flow through their systems. Peter had swallowed his pride from the experience with Cannondale in Brussels and had spent the winter and summer cobbling together the necessary land and water-based technology. He was now supervising a series of tests. For his first test, he had chosen to send a scanned photo of a crotch shot from the Kamasutra to a fellow grad student back in Groningen. Peter hooked up his computer to the water device with three assistants looking on. There was much rejoicing when he hit "Send." Within a minute, the friend in Groningen sent back an email that simply said, "Ouch." It wasn't quite, "Come here, Watson, I need you," but it was good enough for Peter.

They were at the helm of pushing the concept of two

cans and a string out further than anyone ever had. The media had already put them on the cover of *Wired Magazine.* In addition, *BusinessWeek,* the *Financial Times, Le Monde,* and the *Economist* had run major stories. There would be talk shows and girls, and hopefully lots of money. But before any of that could happen, they needed to finish the testing.

The second test involved audio. For this, Peter bought a list of email addresses from a guy who created mailing lists of people who regularly bought CDs online. Peter had contacted them to see if they would participate in the trial in return for free Cheyenne service for a year when the system was fully operational. To his amazement, the majority of them said yes.

The inaugural audio file, T. Rex's "Bang A Gong," was sent to a 20-year-old girl named Karin, who worked in her father's insurance company in Maastricht. "Ladies and gentleman," Peter said as he was about to hit the button, "I give you T. Rex." His assistants tittered. The girl reported having some difficulty detaching the file, which they identified as a problem with her computer.

Dozens of albums followed. They downloaded Elvis collections to a fry cook in Tilburg. They sent Jerry Jeff Walker's "Live at Gruene Hall" to an accountant in Haarlem. They sent John Coltrane's "A Love Supreme" to an artist in Breda. Dvorak's Symphony No. 9, "New World Symphony," went to a builder in Apeldoorn. A secretary in Rotterdam had requested "Trafalgar" by the Brothers Gibb.

Peter guessed that the woman must have just had a bad break up, because that album contained what was, in Peter's mind, one of the better bust up songs of all time: "How Can You Mend A Broken Heart." Peter began to hum as he sent the file and then stopped himself. *Shit, I'm a saddo, he thought..*

He moved on to the next portion of the testing—data. He chose material from authors who tended to write long—Tolstoy, Dostoyevsky, Gibbon, Vidal, Faulkner. Then came the granddaddy of them all—the complete unabridged edition of the Oxford English Dictionary. It worked beautifully, even as a handful of bearded ethical hackers that Peter had contracted attempted to bring down Cheyenne's network.

The final test was video. For this, Peter chose one of his favorite movies of all time—"True Grit" with John Wayne. "It's going to be hard to squeeze a man of the Duke's stature through a water pipe, but here we go," Peter said to one of his assistants. Another assistant began a drum roll. Another made an embarrassing attempt at whooping like a cowboy. "Fill your hand, you son-of-a-bitch," Peter shouted as he hit the button.

It was the kind of moment that geeks live for, and non-geeks shake their heads at. Peter was proud. The conviction he felt began to surge from some darkened place within him. He was pretty sure that he had a hard-on.

They were ready or, at least, getting close. The tests were telling them what they needed to know. The glitches were being addressed, at least, the ones that they could predict. It would only be a matter of time before they were ready to put the first satellite in the sky. The satellite would fill in the gaps in the network where signals could not flow through municipal water supplies, or act as a backup when terrestrial signals failed. Cheyenne's system would not function without a satellite. They needed one fast.

A satellite was important for two other reasons: one, to create the kind of momentum that would make Eatwell and the European Commission think twice before rejecting Lyrical's eventual acquisition of Cheyenne. Two, rumor had it that N-tel, the state-run Dutch telecom carrier, was working hard on a technology that also promised to deliver unlimited bandwidth to the masses, although the scope of its technology was unclear because N-tel was keeping it under tightly-guarded wraps.

Under normal circumstances, it could take a year for delivery of a new satellite. Cheyenne didn't have that kind of time. They needed a satellite now. Aaron could live with a refurbished bird. He told Timmermans to make the necessary calls to get the ball rolling.

Chapter 12

A Swiss banker named Otto Jagmetti, who was fond of wearing bowler hats and fob chains had read about Cheyenne's need for a satellite to fill the bandwidth gaps on its network. He offered his help to Timmermans to secure a Russian-made satellite supplied by a firm called Riga-Tech in Moscow. Riga-Tech had just what they needed—a satellite that had been purchased by another company a year earlier, but the company was having financial problems and had decided against a launch. The satellite was sitting in storage. It was Cheyenne's if they wanted it. Deal.

Timmermans put a down payment on the satellite on behalf of Cannondale. They would pay the rest upon launch. But getting permission to beam signals down to the Netherlands and other parts of Europe was a different story. Civil servants like the Dutch Minister of Waterworks still held the cards on that one.

Gazing out the window of his office near the Paradeplatz onto Lake Zurich, Jagmetti was relishing the middle man deal he had just brokered between three Cold War remnants—an insecure Russia desperate to regain its place in the world, an envious Europe trying to jump start an innovation culture, and a cocky America that still held the marbles.

And in completing the deal, he had also managed to please a new client, one that was so mysterious that Jagmetti referred to him in his own mind only as "the Client." The

Client had expressed a strange interest in knowing when the next communications satellite might be launched over Europe. The Client was precise. He wanted to know when and where. Jagmetti was happy to provide the Client details based on what he knew from his dealings with the Russians and Cheyenne, but he remained curious why the Client wanted to know so much about a communications satellite.

The beautiful thing was that Jagmetti didn't need to ask questions. That wasn't his job. His job was to do what his clients asked of him, keep his head down and get very rich in the process. None of that Anglo, moral claptrap about taking only "clean" clients. What was "clean" anyway? That was a sucker's game. He took all kinds of clients, the same way lawyers did, and he didn't make apologies. Business and morality were mutually exclusive. Morality was for Sundays. Morality was expensive.

A gentle sun danced on the water. The lilies in his office emitted a fresh, clean smell. It was satisfying to be Swiss. He took his coat from the rack, put it on, and walked downstairs. He needed lunch. He decided he'd eat at Cantinella Antinori in the old town near St. Peter's Church. They had excellent veal.

On his way to the restaurant, Jagmetti stopped by Sprungli to get a box of chocolates. Outside of the store, he took a breath of crisp air. He found it difficult to believe that just 200 years ago, they were trading livestock in this fabled square. He was now a true "Zurcher," but it hadn't always been that way. His father came over from Italy in the '50s to work in a turbine plant. His mother was a Swiss-German nurse. They worked hard so that he wouldn't have to, and then they died.

And so, over his veal, Jagmetti quietly toasted his parents with a nice Dole red wine. It seemed the perfect way to congratulate them, and himself.

Chapter 13

Vaughn, it's Aaron Cannondale."

"Aaron, how are you?"

"Fine. Let's get this Cheyenne acquisition rolling. They've completed their IPO; they secured their satellite deal, and they're making good progress. Whadya say?"

"When?"

"Two weeks."

"Two weeks? You sure about that, Aaron? The Euros aren't going to take too kindly to that. They'll think you're pushy."

"I am pushy. Let's do this thing. And let's make a show of it while we're at it. I want this to be so far out there in the public imagination that the Euro-weenies and the folks in Washington can't possibly back away from it."

"Ok, Aaron."

"Are we gonna have any problems with the Justice Department?"

"No."

"Good. Call me when you're ready to pull the trigger. And, oh yeah, Terry. One more thing."

"What's that, Aaron?"

"Let's do it at the Savoy."

"The Savoy in London?"

"Yeah."

"Like the old days?"

"You got it."

"Why the Savoy, Aaron?"

"I always liked those little sandwiches without the crusts that they serve at high tea."

Chapter 14

The Netherlands is about twice the size of New Jersey. It's essentially a delta comprised of silt from the mouths of the Rhine, Waal, Maas, IJssel and Scheldt rivers. The average elevation of the country is 36 feet. When a plane lands at the Amsterdam airport, Schiphol, it is hitting the runway at about ten feet below sea level.

The 12th province of the Netherlands, a place called Flevoland, was carved out of the sea. It is considered one of the Seven Wonders of the Modern World by the American Society of Civil Engineers.

And so, Elliott Pettigrew—part pitbull, part lobbyist, part Louisiana good ol' boy, and Aaron's man in Washington—thought it fitting that the Netherlands was the birthplace of Cheyenne.

Aaron had sent Pettigrew to Amsterdam to meet with Kuipers at the Ministry of Waterworks. Aaron thought it wouldn't hurt to butter up the Dutchman before Lyrical and Cheyenne made the acquisition public.

Tech rags had spilled endless ink about Cheyenne's technology. European futurists were brimming with excitement about the impending possibilities of unlimited bandwidth delivered, not by thousands of miles of unused fiber that had been hastily put in the ground by the world's telecom companies, but rather through a completely new and promising technology. Meanwhile, the rumors about the Dutch national telephone company, N-tel, developing a type of rival technology continued to swirl despite the fact that Cheyenne's technology was considered to be in a league of its own.

Even before Cannondale had become interested in Cheyenne, Timmermans and Peter had secured Kuipers' permission to use the Dutch national water system to send data on a trial basis—a decision for which Kuipers still punished himself. Kuipers hadn't really understood Cheyenne's technology. He thought he was helping the small Dutch company get a head start. But of course, that was all before Cannondale entered the picture.

Now, the headlines blared about how Cheyenne had secured a satellite. The upstart was on its way. But what was done could be undone. Kuipers had the power to be a kingmaker, and like Eatwell, he sure as hell had no intention of crowning Cannondale.

Kuipers' Amsterdam office was located at 156 Beatrixstraat. The lobby was a combination of brushed steel, pine tables, trendy halogen lamps, and fresh tulips. "Euro-crap," Pettigrew muttered under his breath.

"*Meneer?*" a short-haired, middle-aged woman said from behind the lobby desk.

"Elliot Pettigrew to see Mr. Kuipers, please."

She picked up a phone, whispered something into it, hung it up, and pointed to the elevators with an attitude that grated on him. He couldn't pinpoint what it was that he disliked about her. It was a sort of continental arrogance he sometimes felt when he was in Europe.

"Third floor," she said sternly.

"You don't get laid much, do you?" Pettigrew mumbled incomprehensibly, turning to enter the elevator.

Pettigrew took a seat in Kuipers' waiting room. It couldn't have been more different from the lobby. It had an old-school, Napoleonic grandeur that momentarily sent Pettigrew back to the big houses of his childhood in New Orleans. On one wall was a framed copy of Vermeer's "The Art of the Painting." Another painting was filled with Rubenesque nymphs frolicking near a pond with a grinning goat in the background. *Not bad,* Pettigrew thought.

He could just see into Kuipers' office from where he was sitting. There were urns, and ornate corbels on faux pillars midway up the walls. In the corners stood busts of August European statesmen.

Another stern woman, maybe the receptionist's sister, arrived to offer Pettrigrew coffee. "Black, please," he said.

He picked up a copy of the *Financial Times* from the coffee table just as a figure appeared in the office doorway.

"Mr. Pettigrew?" It was Kuipers.

"Please, come in, Mr. Pettigrew, sit down."

"Thank you."

"I trust you had a good trip?"

"I did."

"Good. Now, before we begin, I must tell you that I am not a fan of your Mr. Cannondale."

"Oh?"

"No, I'm not. And if you're thinking of leaking that to

the press, I'll just deny it."

"May I ask why you have formed this opinion?" "No, you may not."

"In that case, you're not going to like what I've come here to talk to you about."

Kuipers remained expressionless.

"You are aware of Cheyenne's intention to use satellites to fill out its network. We have made arrangements to supply Cheyenne with an initial bird."

"Who is *we*, Mr. Pettigrew?"

"I beg your pardon?"

"*We.* You refer to *we.* I ask because it has never been entirely clear to me what your role is in Cheyenne's affairs."

"*We* is Cheyenne, whom I represent, Mr. Kuipers." "Are you an employee of Cheyenne?"

"Cheyenne has hired me as a consultant."

"But you are also a consultant for Aaron Cannondale and Lyrical, Inc., yes?"

"I am."

"Mr. Cannondale appears to be quite anxious to help Cheyenne move ahead with the build-out of its infrastructure."

"Well, the company is young. I don't necessarily consider that rushing things."

"I would have thought that a businessman as savvy as Mr. Cannondale would understand the notion of patience in these types of affairs."

"Patience?"

"Let me put it bluntly, Mr. Pettigrew. I do not like Mr. Cannondale."

"You mentioned that."

"I like neither his arrogance, nor his presumption that because Cheyenne has received our blessing to conduct trials here in the Netherlands that he somehow has carte blanche with the future of this endeavor. I understand the American affinity toward getting things done quickly, Mr. Pettigrew, but on this matter, I would advise that Lyrical err more on the side of delayed gratification than immediate conquest."

Pettigrew fumed, but he caught himself before he spoke. "Sir, you are absolutely right. That's sound advice. I apologize for my abruptness. I know I can speak for all the principals at Cheyenne when I say that we are grateful for the opportunity to conduct our trials in the Netherlands. I think we all understand how potentially important this technology is. We have every intention of proceeding within the parameters laid out by the Dutch government."

"It is reassuring to hear that, Mr. Pettigrew."

"I can also speak for Mr. Cannondale when I say that he is anxious to work with the Dutch government on any steps that can be taken to ensure Cheyenne's success, a success that Mr. Cannondale is eager to share with the Dutch people. On a larger political level, we are, of course, well aware that the last few years haven't necessarily been a high point in the transatlantic relationship, but the economic foundation of US/EU relations remains sound. Our view is that the more partnering we can do together on common interests the better both of our peoples will fare. You are aware of Mr. Cannondale's recent plans to donate a new research facility in Utrecht?"

"I am. Very timely, I'd have to say."

"In the interest of understanding one another then, we would like to secure satellite broadcasting rights in the Netherlands to fill out Cheyenne's network. We have secured such rights from other members of the EU. Failure to expand with satellites will not only jeopardize Cheyenne's current trial but ultimately its ability to provide services once the trial has ended."

"What are you proposing?"

"Cheyenne would soon like to launch a satellite—its first. Doing so will allow us to maintain our timelines. Our client base will initially be pan-Europe, but as you know, we must secure satellite rights from administrators such as yourself in each country where we wish to broadcast signals. I might add that Cheyenne's plans are also consistent with your prime minister's push, as well as the European Commission's efforts, to promote an innovation agenda."

"Our prime minister's push is meant to promote innovation between European Union members, Mr. Pettigrew. You're from Louisiana, are you not?"

"I am. How is that relevant?"

"I just have to think that if someone in the city of New

Orleans had discovered Cheyenne's technology, and a wealthy man from the Netherlands showed up to take it over ... excuse me, to buy a controlling stake, how would the fair citizens of New Orleans feel about that?"

"The people of New Orleans may be southern, sir, but that does not preclude them from being good capitalists. They would understand."

"Would they?"

"Mr. Kuipers. Can we stick to the point of our meeting?"

"Of course."

"It's my understanding that your prime minister's push for an innovation agenda is primarily, but *not* exclusively, focused on activities within the EU, or has that changed?"

"Mr. Pettigrew, what is it that Mr. Cannondale and Cheyenne want exactly?"

"What any good business wants—to profit. Can Cheyenne count on your approval to let it use satellite technology to fill out its network?"

"Regrettably, although I have not yet come to a final decision, you cannot count on my approval at this moment in time," Kuipers said. The statement didn't surprise Pettigrew considering Kuipers' cold reception, but the bluntness did. He expected some equivocation, some room for discussion. "May I ask why not?"

"Because although Mr. Cannondale now owns a portion of Cheyenne, any future increase in that shareholding would have the potential to dominate Internet communications in the Netherlands. Capitalism isn't a particularly American endeavor, Mr. Pettigrew. We understand the concept of competition quite well."

"I see. I was under the impression that given the good work that Cheyenne had already undertaken in this country the ministry would be partial to helping see the project through to completion."

"That's presumptuous."

"Is that a formal 'no'?"

"For the time being."

"In that case, sir, I thank you for your time, and I look forward to revisiting this in the near future."

"By all means," Kuipers said.

With that, the two men shook hands. Pettigrew smiled and left. Round One.

Chapter 15

Hayden had just finished putting the final touches on a speech for Aaron, who was sitting across from him in the cabin of the Gulfstream doing a crossword puzzle.

Hayden's head ached from staring at the laptop. He closed his eyes to take a nap. Just as he was about to drift off to sleep, the phone rang. Aaron put it on speaker phone:

"Aaron, it's Elliot."

Elliot Pettigrew, Hayden thought. *Aaron's Washington guy.*

"Elliot. Good to hear from you. How did it go with the water miser?" Aaron said, laying down the crossword.

"Not well, Aaron. This whole Iraq thing has got the Euros spooked. It's the backdrop to every conversation they have about the United States. They're so pissed off they can't think straight. Beyond that though, I think something else is going on."

"Like what?"

"I think somebody has gotten to Kuipers. He's stiff-arming us."

"What do you mean?"

"My guess, he's stalling until the Dutch telecom company, N-tel, can catch up on this type of technology."

"N-tel? They're a joke. Do they really think they have a chance?"

"They have the Dutch government on their side. I've got a guy inside over there, Aaron. He did some digging.

They're definitely looking to roll-out some sort of service down the road."

"Nothing like Cheyenne's, right?"

"Not even close. My guy says they are stumbling in the dark."

"I could have told you that, Elliot. It's going to take them years."

"Maybe, Aaron, but these Europeans have a way of protecting the home team, if you know what I mean. This guy Kuipers likes the stage, Aaron. He's smitten by the limelight. He's got fucking busts of Metternich in his office, for God's sake. He's basically denying us permission to use the satellite over the Netherlands, at least for now."

"What an idiot."

"Nonetheless, Aaron, he's pretty firm on this."

"It's me."

"What's you, Aaron?"

"They can't stand the fact that an American wants to foot the bill."

"That is a problem, Aaron. It has been from the beginning. They don't like guys like you. You're as toxic as Bush. Makes them crazy."

"Have you talked to Vaughn over at Teestone yet?"

"No. I think Timmermans has though."

"Get on the phone with them, Elliot." Aaron looked over at Hayden, who was feigning sleep with his eyes closed. Hayden could feel Aaron's eyes on him.

"Tell Vaughn to get moving on the announcement,

Elliot. We're going to have to crowd out Mr. Kuipers on this. I don't care what it takes. It's just hard to believe."

"What is?"

"That these guys are willing to sacrifice what is inherently good for their own people for the sake of trying to act as a counterweight to the United States. Typical European pettiness."

"It makes them feel relevant, I suppose."

"Get on the phone with Vaughn. If there's anyone who can push this through quickly, it's Vaughn—Vaughn and Braun. Clear your calendar, Elliot. We're going to London."

Chapter 16

The press release hit the wires at 8:00 a.m. on Thursday, December 15, 2005, New York time to give the Street time to digest it before the opening bell at 9:30.

For Immediate Release:

Lyrical, Inc. Buys Cheyenne B.V. for $300 Million

A New Generation of Bandwidth Services; Provides Unlimited Voice, Video, Data Through Municipal Water Systems; Fastest Connection Speeds in the World.

Salt Lake City, Utah, and Amsterdam, The Netherlands – Lyrical, Inc. (NASDAQ) acquired the outstanding shares of Cheyenne B.V. in an all-cash deal worth $300 million, which represents a 36% premium over yesterday's closing price.

Subject to completion of the transaction and regulatory approval, Cheyenne, a global leader in communications solutions, will become a media and entertainment arm of Lyrical, Inc.

"The technology that Cheyenne is developing offers a rare glimpse of the future," said Lyrical President, Richard Blyth. "Soon, the complaints about bandwidth limitations will be a problem of the past."

"Lyrical brings us the kind of breadth and scale that we need at this point," said Cheyenne CEO, Phillipe Timmermans. "Most important, our shareholders will benefit from increased synergies with one of the world's true technology powerhouses."

Cheyenne is the world's only provider of a highly secretive technology it has developed called "STS" or "Seamless Transmission System," which allows consumers to send and receive voice, video and data through water pipes in their homes.

Teestone Financial will act as dealer manager for the offer in the United States and as financial adviser to Lyrical. For further information about the offer, please contact Joseph Schwartz or Terence McDonald at Teestone Financial at +212.472.4376.

* * * *

"Just the first volley," Aaron beamed as he read the release on his laptop in his suite at the Savoy. Gathered around him were Pettigrew, Timmermans, Peter, Vaughn, and Cheyenne's CFO, Michelle. And then there was Hayden—Aaron's newly minted Director of Communications. He felt like a tagalong.

"This dog is definitely gonna hunt," Pettigrew said, patting Aaron on the back.

"Okay, Vaughn, why don't you give us the rundown of what to expect today," Aaron said.

Vaughn gave Aaron a perplexed look. "Aaron, I know it's been a couple of years since anybody has been buying anything, but you've been through acquisitions a hundred times. You know the drill."

"Of course I do, Vaughn, but I thought it might be nice if you explained it to some of the virgins among us today," Aaron said, looking over at Hayden and Peter, then breaking into a broad smile. Everyone laughed.

"Well, it's quite simple. Aaron, you will make the announcement and then do a Q&A. We'll keep it short and sweet."

Pettigrew nodded excitedly, as did Timmermans.

"Then you and Timmermans will do a splash of interviews—BBC, CNN, all the wires, the FT, *The New York Times*, the *Journal*, *De Telegraaf* and *NRC Handelsblad* from the Netherlands, and a handful of other European newspapers."

"Not *Le Monde,* right?" Pettigrew said. "Waste of time. Those guys can't stand us."

"No *Le Monde*, that is correct."

"And we're not granting any interviews to that Belgian rag," Pettigrew said. "What's the name of it again, Timmermans?"

"*Le Soir.*"

"That's right, *Le Sewer*," Pettigrew said, intentionally mangling the name.

"It's pronounced SOIRE, Elliot," Timmermans repeated. The others laughed.

"SOIRE, SEWER, who gives a damn?"

Timmermans shook his head. He didn't have much

time for Pettigrew.

"After the interviews, it's really nothing more than a big party," Vaughn continued, "which will last until about noon, at which time, Aaron, you've got a brief lunch with Branson over at Virgin."

"Love that guy," Aaron said.

"Snap a few more pictures, shake a few more hands, thank everyone, and then we're off to New York to do it all over again for an American audience."

"Man, if they still flew the Rocket we'd be back in New York in a few hours. What the hell were they thinking getting rid of it?" Pettigrew said.

"The *rocket*?" Hayden asked.

"The Concorde," Aaron explained. "That's how we used to do these kinds of things—spend the morning in London, fly back to New York the same day in time for another dog and pony show followed by martinis at Sparks."

"I miss that," Pettigrew said nostalgically. "So do I, Elliot," Aaron said."

"Sounds good," Vaughn said, straightening his tie. "Let's do it." They gathered their things and made their way to the hallway, pairing up and chatting as they left. Michelle kept to herself, as she often did. Hayden was intrigued. He'd been intrigued since they first met at the restaurant in Brussels where Aaron laid out his conquest of Cheyenne.

Aaron and Vaughn huddled together on the far side of the room. Hayden paused awkwardly, not knowing whether or not he should wait for them. He made eye contact with Aaron, who shot back an emotionless stare that left Hayden cold. Aaron's face said, "You're excused."

Peter, who was standing next to Hayden, leaned over and whispered, "This is going to be a circus."

Pettigrew, whom Peter hadn't noticed behind him, slapped him on the back and said, "Midgets and all, my friend, midgets and all."

Chapter 17

A pious-looking old man with a skull cap and flowing robes made his way through the early morning scrimmage of the Old City section of Sana'a.

The Yemeni sun burned away a cold mountain mist and brought to life the earth-colored houses of the ancient place. The old man carried the traditional Yemeni jambiya dagger at his waist.

The marketplace was in full regalia. Guttural voices haggled over lambs, dried fish, mint, tomatoes, onion tops, and mangoes. Arms flailed. Women in raspberry-colored shawls laughed and gossiped as carriers from Wadi Dhahr and other surrounding areas transported bundles of qat, Yemen's universal stimulant, on their heads. In the distance, the great old friend known as Mount Nuqum put its arms around the citizens of Sana'a, as it did every day, as it had forever.

The old man passed through the market quickly, taking little notice of the sounds and smells around him. He crossed a cobblestone street as a young boy encouraged two goats to walk through a wooden door leading to the first floor of his family's house. The street rose to a tiny square where more goats milled around unattended. The man came to a house, looked around, and went in.

The first thing he smelled as he entered the house was horse dung. Not many people kept animals in their homes anymore but that's where they kept "Tulsa" —the skinny filly that the young inhabitants of the house bought upon their return from the United States. Tulsa looked to see who was there.

"*Kayfa halik*? (How are you?)," the old man said quietly, extending his hand to her muzzle.

Tulsa snorted and bowed her head to smell the man's palm. The man patted the animal, then climbed the stairs to the first floor. This room had a sweet smell of coffee, tobacco, and dried goods. It was the storage floor. He went up to the second floor. There was a diwan, a sitting room for guests. Breathing hard, he climbed to the third floor where he found the two young men tapping furiously at their keyboards.

Colorful rugs and stuffed cushions lined the room. Incense burned in a metal bowl.

A copy of the Koran rested upon a rosewood stand in the corner. Around the outline of the window that looked onto the city was an aqd—a plaster molding with leaves and flowers and the name "Allah" deeply etched in it.

"*As-salaam alaikum*," the man said to the younger men.

"*Wa alaikum as-salaam*," they repeated perfunctorily, keeping their eyes on their computer screens. To them, the old man was a teacher of sorts, a mentor.

Yemen was not home to any of the three men, but it served them well. The country had always been a crossroads of sorts. It was both a frontier and a metropolis. Most important for the old man and his two disciples, Yemen took the traditional Islamic sacredness of hospitality to heart. It was the sort of place that didn't readily give up its secrets.

"I'm in," Nabil, the youngest and the most talented of the two young men, said excitedly, tapping at his computer.

"Where are they on the list?" his partner, Hassan, asked.

"Step twenty-seven."

"That's good," said the old man.

"We've spaced them out; we'll add the patch somewhere between steps thirty-three and forty-seven," Nabil said.

The old man nodded, pleased.

Nabil and Hassan had known each other since they were six years old in Pakistan. More than friends, they had been classmates at one of that country's better-known madrassas—sent there by their parents who wanted something more for the boys than the toil and despair that had been a fixture of their own lives.

At the madrassa, the boys relentlessly recited the Koran and lived a simple life devoted to Islamic learning, self-reliance, and absolute devotion to Allah. Initially, Nabil and Hassan disliked the madrassa—so strict, so stern, so entirely foreign from the laughter they remembered in their homes. Later, they came to understand the wisdom of their parents and embraced the teachings willingly.

The madrassa had prepared them for dealing with Allah, with hunger, with women and temptation. Neither Nabil nor Hassan could point to America on the map when the old man had offered to pay for their education in, of all places, America. Their parents were initially against it, but the old man had convinced them of the merits of his charity. Besides, the boys wouldn't be gone long.

"It is near," the old man said. He unfurled a carpet from the corner of the room, placed it on the ground and prostrated himself. "It is near."

Chapter 18

Somewhere in the mix of jet fuel and asphalt at the Salt Lake City International Airport, Hayden was pretty sure he smelled sage.

He was greeted by one of Aaron's drivers in a black Lincoln Town Car. London was behind them now. Wall Street was pleased by the much-needed injection that Cheyenne was giving to the market. The stories had been written and the company's stock was soaring, as was Commissioner Eatwell's blood pressure.

Hayden had heard from Pettigrew that Eatwell had been primed to call a press conference the same day that the deal was announced, but that he was talked out of it by his staff who thought that it would be interpreted as defensive.

Aaron had ticked the Euros off something fierce, but it didn't seem to bother him. In fact, Aaron did what he often did when he stared adversity in the face and came out smiling—he sent out party invitations. Hayden felt compelled to attend.

The car pulled through the gate and onto the half-mile stretch of road leading up to Kshanti. Along the way, gardeners and landscapers turned their heads to see who it was. It was sunny, about 76 degrees. Orthanel, Aaron's manservant, waited at the door. He was one of Hayden's favorite fixtures of Kshanti, mainly because he was so out of place. Orthanel was from one of those isolated sea islands on the Carolina coast where blacks still spoke Gullah, an archaic almost Elizabethan form of English mixed with Creole and a few West African dialects. His father had been a sharecropper. Orthanel picked cotton, too, until someone suggested that he put his face to use in the movies. So he did. He played bit parts—slaves, Indians, clowns, drunks, Uncle Toms, shoeshine boys, shrimpers, Egyptians, and butlers. And yet he was never really discovered.

"Mr. Hayden, how you been?"

"Not bad, Orthanel. You?"

"Not bad, not bad at all. Thanks for askin', but I got the gout in my big toe."

"Ouch. What are you doing for it?"

"Doctor gave me some pills, but they ain't workin'. Chocolate fudge ice cream seems to help," Orthenel said with a smile that slowly broadened across his face. "Mr. Cannondale is expecting you. He has house guests. I'll bring you to him."

"Not necessary, Orthanel, I know the way. China Room?"

"Yes, sir."

Hayden walked through two broad hallways to a thick wooden door which led outside to the cloisters—possibly his favorite place in Kshanti. Aaron had brought them over, stone by stone, from an abandoned monastery in the south of France. At the center of the cloisters was a Biblical garden where Aaron had the gardener plant flora specifically mentioned in the good book. Aaron wasn't the least bit religious; he just liked the concept of having a l garden.

Hayden walked slowly. There was an apricot tree, which, as Aaron had once explained to him, was thought by some scholars to have been the fabled fruit that Adam ate, not the apple. There were figs, which Adam and Eve used to clothe themselves when they were embarrassed by their nakedness. There were lentils, which Jacob used to swindle his older brother Esau out of his birthright as oldest son. There were onions, garlic, coriander, tamarisk, sage, globe thistle, and castor beans.

Hayden remembered somewhere that Isaiah declared judgment upon those who fashioned idols out of the wood of the bay laurel tree. Sure enough, there was bay laurel. There was also barley to represent the loaves that Jesus converted, along with fish, into a meal for the multitude. There was a good looking palm tree to represent Jesus' entry into Jerusalem as the Messiah. There were centaurea plants, relatives of the thorns that were made into Jesus' crown. There was aloe that was used to anoint Jesus' body after the crucifixion, and finally, there were poppies, the same kind that grew outside of Jesus' tomb.

Hayden's favorite plants in the garden were hollyhock and mallow. They harkened back to Job. Satan had tested Job. Of the many hardships that Job endured, one was the loss of appetite. In Job's time, hollyhock and mallow were used to flavor foods. The modern descendant of hollyhock and mallow is the marshmallow.

Hayden walked through the courtyard into the room where Aaron was entertaining. Aaron loved having people out to Kshanti. His parties were legendary. One Christmas, he'd had a heated big top tent raised on the property and flew in one of Spain's top matadors, who successfully felled a bull.

When it came to the guests at his parties, Aaron amused himself with a game he called "Guest of Honor." It had become a bit of an Aaron trademark on the soiree circuit. He would designate someone to be his guest of honor for that particular evening; only he wouldn't tell anyone. They all had to guess. Aaron's criteria for being considered an honored guest varied. Sometimes it was about social position. Other times it was about intellect. Sometimes it was a person who made Aaron laugh. Sometimes it was about clinching a deal. Other times it was about sizing up an enemy.

Aaron beamed as soon as Hayden walked in, throwing up his hands as if to say, "Where ya been?" He motioned Hayden to come over to a circle of people.

"Hayden, I'd like you to meet some folks. This is Utah Senator, Emily Van Horn."

She was in her mid-50s. *Hmm, a senator*, Hayden thought to himself. *Good candidate for guest of honor.* Van Horn had the same safe, durable coif that most female American politicians resort to at some point in their careers. She also had a particularly strong voice on the U.S. Senate's Committee on Commerce, Science, and Transportation. Aaron liked her because she liked him, *and* because she was his most influential unpaid lobbyist in the Senate. *Nope, she's not it.* Hayden decided.

Aaron made a few more introductions, then excused himself to take care of another group. Hayden shook hands with a local businessman named J.D. Langhorn, a man who had managed to make millions during the dot.com boom, lose it, and then make a bundle selling coffins fashioned from chicken feces.

"Chicken shit, who woulda thought?" Langhorn bragged, chewing a large, unlit cigar. "I got the idea from something I read. A couple of Germans had tried to do the same thing. Naturally, the German government got involved and put all kinds of restrictions on them 'til they suffocated the business."

Gotta love American luck and pluck, Hayden thought to himself. This guy had all the markings of guest of honor.

"How do you sell people on the concept?" Hayden asked, incredulous. "I mean, given the choice between pine and chicken feces, isn't it kind of clear which one most people would prefer to bury Uncle Fred in?"

"Uncle Fred has left the building, know what I mean, Bo?" Langhorn said, grinning. "What does Fred care? And if Fred gave one red cent about the environment, he'd pick chicken shit, I guarantee it. You know how much chicken shit this country produces each year?"

"Nope."

"A lot. Stuff's like nuclear waste. They don't know what to do with it."

"Who are *they*?"

"Federal government. They want to have their cake and eat it, too."

Hayden couldn't believe that he had uncovered the mystery guest so quickly. "What do you mean?" he asked, entertained.

"They encouraged people to eat chicken because it was healthy. Spent all kinds of money on advertising, gave subsidies to the chicken farmers so they could put birds on everybody's kitchen table, but they don't have a clue what to do with the waste. They don't want to think about it. They tried to sell it to the Peruvians or some such place last year—very hush hush—but those guys didn't even want it. That's when I swooped down on this idea to sell my coffins on the Web."

"Do you sell many of them?" "Forty-five a week."

"What?" Hayden said loudly, surprised.

Aaron returned and whisked him away to another group. "Enjoying yourself, Hayden?" Aaron asked, taking him by the arm.

"It's a good party, Aaron."

"There's a ton of book material at this gathering tonight, Hayden—loads. Make sure you take good notes."

"Will do."

"Chris, I'd like you to meet Hayden Campbell, my speechwriter. 'Mr. Original,' that's what I call him. The guy has a river of ideas. Hayden, this is Chris Babcock; he's one of the survivors. Started three successful dot.coms. The guy knows how to write a business plan, and how to raise money.

"By the way, Langhorn isn't it," Aaron whispered in Hayden's ear as he moved on.

"... So then I decided to sell that start up and move onto this one," Babcock babbled as Hayden refocused his attention on the conversation.

"What kind of start up?" Hayden asked, sipping a bourbon and ginger, filling the dead air, not hugely interested.

"It's not that sexy, really."

"Try me."

"Well, it helps dot.com meltdowns sell their office equipment. Someone's got to do the cleanup, know what I mean?"

Nice, Hayden thought, smiling at Babcocks' charitableness. The guy even looked like a carrion eater—bloodshot eyes, a beakish nose, and bad posture that made him appear as though he was hovering over you. *Guest of honor? No way.* Babcock reminded Hayden of a turkey vulture he'd once seen on the side of the road in West Virginia picking at a deer that had been hit by a car.

"You ought to meet that gentleman there," Hayden said, raising his glass to point to Langhorn. "Will you excuse me?"

Hayden made his way to a table of hors d'oeuvres. A short guy with a bad tie was shoving a piece of pita bread covered with hummus into his mouth. The paste oozed onto the back of his hand. He licked it off. The man smiled, cut off a hunk of pâté, grabbed a gherkin, dumped the

102

concoction onto a sesame cracker and jammed it in his mouth. Hayden wondered whether or not the hummus had fully made it down the hatch before the pâté was introduced. It was as if the man hadn't eaten in three days. Noticing the horrified look on Hayden's face, the man took a napkin, wiped his hand, and extended it.

"Tom Feegan."

"Hayden Campbell."

"You a friend of Cannondale's?"

The question made Hayden think. "I suppose you could say that."

"Kind of a whack job, don't you think?"

Hayden was amused. "How so?"

"This house for a start. Who builds something like this in Utah? What the hell is Utah, anyway? You know how freaking hard it is to get out here?"

"How do you know Aaron?"

"I don't. He just invites me to these things every once in a while to ply me with imported beer and chicks in hopes that I'll write good things about him."

"You're a journalist?" Hayden said, slightly surprised that Aaron would invite the media to such an event.

"Yes," Feegan said, manhandling a hunk of Stilton onto a piece of toast. He spoke with his mouth full. "I freelance. I've been trying to do a piece on this Dutch company that Cannondale is trying to buy—pending regulatory approval, of course."

"I see."

Aaron appeared from nowhere behind them. "Ah, I see the two men of words have met." Feegan looked puzzled.

"Feegan, you've got a ways to go before you hit this guy's level," Aaron said, slapping Hayden's back.

"Hell of a way to flatter a reporter, Aaron."

"Oh, I'm not worried about that. Somehow you always seem to find the good in things, Has Hayden introduced himself? He can be bashful."

"We were just getting to that," Hayden said.

"What did he tell you he did for a living, Tom? I'm curious."

"I just got his name; that's all."

"What kind of reporter are you, Feegan? I thought it was 'who, what, when, where, why, and how' within the first 30 seconds?"

"'Must be off my game."

"Hayden here is my Director of Communications, and also my speechwriter. 'Mr. Original,' that's what I call him. The guy has a way."

"Interesting."

"Anyway, you guys probably have a lot in common. I'll leave you to it."

Leave us to what exactly? Hayden wondered.

"Oh, by the way, Hayden," Aaron said in a hushed tone. "I'll talk to you about that 'thing' later." Aaron gave Hayden a devilish look as he left.

"So you play Cyrano to Aaron Cannondale, huh?" Feegan said, somewhat sarcastically. "What's that like?"

"I don't know."

"Is he an asshole? I've heard he can be. A lot of these guys like him can be. You know, this could be an interesting story in itself—the voice behind Aaron Cannondale. The guy who keeps him on cue. Whadya think?"

"Not a good idea," Hayden said, annoyed that for one, Aaron would even invite this guy to his party to pick over random conversations by some pretty high-level people; and two, that Aaron had opened the door to this kind of scrutiny. It was reckless, and Aaron knew it. But what galled Hayden most was that Aaron seemed to have done it deliberately.

"So what's this 'thing' Aaron just asked you about?" Feegan asked.

"I don't know."

"Come on, guy. You're his speechwriter. I know you don't know me from Adam, but throw me a bone here."

"I'm serious. I don't know what he's talking about."

Feegan gave Hayden an incredulous smile. "Okay, pal, I can respect that, but if you ever want to talk, give me a shout. Here's my card."

"I'll keep it in mind."

Feegan walked away to eavesdrop on another conversation. Maybe Feegan was a plant. Maybe Aaron staged the whole thing to assess Hayden's loyalty. If so, Hayden was not happy. Life was too short for those kinds of games. Hayden didn't like feeling like he was some sort of pawn.

He made his way to the other side of the room where a portion of Aaron's art collection hung on a burgundy-colored wall. A Chinese oil painting caught his eye. The subject was a solitary, rural Chinese farmer with a puffed-up face. He wore a black peasant outfit. His hands and feet were tiny. The plaque on the wall next to the painting read: "Youth."

"I like it," a man standing next to Hayden said. "Grotesque, yet funny in a way. It's one of his better works."

"Who?"

"The artist, Pan Dehai. He spent ten years painting farmers like this. They were people he knew when he lived in Kunming. A lot of people compare him to Botero."

"Youth?" Hayden said, looking at the painting. "I suppose he's saying that it's all been sapped out of this guy."

"That's probably the general idea. Who's to say?"

"You know a lot about art."

"I should, I'm surrounded by it every day. I'm sorry, I haven't introduced myself. My name is Thomas Mason. I'm the guest of honor," Mason said with a wink. "You thought it was chicken man over there, didn't you? Legitimate mistake."

Hayden laughed. Mason's name sounded familiar, as if he should know it. Just then, Aaron walked up and gave Hayden a wink.

"Ah, Hayden, I see you have met possibly the world's only remaining Renaissance man. Thomas has the best job going. One of the best kept secrets."

"What do you do?" Hayden asked sheepishly, feeling that he should already know.

"He's the U.S. Ambassador to the Vatican," Aaron volunteered.

"I wouldn't mind being that when I grow up," Hayden said.

"What do I need to do now to prepare?"

"Go to church, give money, write a couple of books, be a Eucharistic minister, I don't know. In my case, the current administration didn't know where else to put me. Somebody found out that I could sing the words to "Nessun Dorma" in Italian, and I guess it was settled. Will you excuse me for a moment? There's someone I must say hello to."

"Good man," Aaron said of Mason. "And modest. I meant it when I said the guy is a Renaissance man. He paints, writes, and is a leading authority on the Etruscan language. He managed to do all that while making a fortune on Wall Street trading derivatives."

"And he's the guest of honor."

"Good man, Hayden. You figured it out."

"Not really. He told me."

"I'll have to reprimand him."

"Aaron, can I ask you something?"

"Of course."

"What was that over there a moment ago with Feegan?"

"What do you mean?"

107

"Was that some sort of test?"

"Test?"

"Feegan grilled me. What did you expect him to do? If you doubt my loyalty for some reason, Aaron, then we've got a problem, and this isn't the place to talk about it. I've told you before that 'kiss and tell' isn't my game."

Aaron let Hayden vent.

"Two things, Aaron. If it was a test, I don't appreciate it. If it wasn't, you still shouldn't have done it."

"Point taken, my friend. Won't happen again."

Somehow Hayden doubted Aaron's sincerity. Aaron took Hayden by the arm to introduce him to others.

"One more thing, Aaron."

"Jeez, I said I was sorry, Hayden."

"No, not that. Do you ever get tired of all this?"

"Tired of what?"

"The show. I mean you always seem to make a point of being 'on.'"

"I guess it depends on the light in which you view it. When you're not on, you're off, know what I mean? I can't imagine it any other way. Some guys watch baseball. Some guys drink. Some guys chase women. My father did all three. The man wasted his life, Hayden."

"What did he do?"

"He was an inventor. He built things. When he came over from Tbilisi, he was fired up. Changed our family name to Cannondale to sound more 'Anglo.' He was going to make a whole new life for himself. Was going to stop at nothing. Wasn't going to let anyone get in his way. Then he met my mother. She was from North Carolina. Pretty thing. I've seen pictures of the two of them together when they were young. He made her laugh; she let him touch her. You know how it goes. They got married, had me, worked hard. But that wasn't enough for my father. It's not enough for any thinking man, which he was. When he wasn't building, he was reading stuff, all kinds of stuff. She began to stifle him. She nagged and wore him down. She sucked the youth and the fire right out of him, or, at least, that's his story. And you know once you lose that fire it's virtually impossible to retrieve it."

"He never blamed himself?"

"Sure, but it's always easier to blame it on a woman, isn't it? Truth is, it was a combination of his giving up and her crushing him. I swore to myself that I'd never lose that fire, no matter who or what was sacrificed. Life is too short, Hayden."

"Too short for what?"

"Too short for regrets, or brooding, or nostalgia, or all the other ingredients that kill men. Too short for errors. I don't like errors, Hayden. That's why it pays to do your homework—as he does," Aaron said, pointing over to Braun.

"Braun, the analyst?"

"The guy is ice, Hayden. Nothing flusters him. That's because he doesn't leave himself open. No errors with that guy, just straight ahead, no-nonsense money making. And

Vaughn there. He's the same. The guys from Teestone are solid. It pays to work with folks who look out for you, my friend—folks who have your best interest in mind, who will take care of you before they take care of others. Do you understand what I mean?"

"I do, Aaron."

"It's all about having your boys in place, Hayden. You know, there are a thousand things out there that can kill you — pancreatic cancer, heart attack, a bullet, a guy behind the wheel with a blood alcohol level that would have felled Fatty Arbuckle. And then there are errors. Errors kill, Hayden, remember that. But you know what worries me the most?"

"No, what?"

"What worries me most is that you can do your best to avoid the external things, but there's something sinister about your own mind turning on you, about giving up. That's what happened to my father. It's not happening to me. That's why Cheyenne is so important, Hayden. It's fresh. It's new. It's alive. It's the most important project I've got going."

For most men, an undertaking like Cheyenne would be the biggest thing in their lives. For Aaron, it was a "project." Hayden found himself looking around the room. Aaron's soothing voice floated in and out. Langhorn—the chicken man—cackled with someone in the corner. Chris Babcock—the survivor—had that schizophrenic look of confidence and fear that people get when they know they've squeaked by. Mason—the ambassador—pondered another canvas.

Important people were about, but for a fleeting moment there was an absence of mystique. It was a canvas of smiles and handshakes and backslapping that always seemed to look good in the right kind of lighting, regardless of the decade. But it was also as if a camera shutter had opened and closed in a split second, and in that second Hayden could see every blemish, every look of fear out of the corner of the eyes of the confident, every desperate attempt to recreate the blip of unprecedented prosperity the world was unlikely to ever see again. Hayden wondered how it would all look tomorrow without the halogen glow. Aaron's world was larger than life. Part of Hayden wanted to shun it, but he couldn't help but embrace it.

"I better get going," Hayden said.

"So soon?" Aaron said. "You disappoint me."

"I have an early morning. I've gotta make you look good, Aaron."

"Good man. Have Orthanel show you to your guest room. I'll see you for breakfast."

Hayden made his way toward the door. Before he left, he turned to have one last look around the room. He noticed Aaron catch the eye of Vaughn, who was chatting in the corner with a nubile blonde—one of the handful of modeling agency girls that Aaron regularly flew out from New York to beautify his parties. Aaron motioned for Vaughn to follow him into a wood-paneled side room.

111

What's that all about? Hayden wondered. Aaron caught Hayden's eye and winked as he and Terry Vaughn went into the side room. The door closed slowly.

Chapter 19

Timmermans, Michelle, and Peter were very different now than they were before the London and New York trips. They could not believe how well the events had gone. Confidence was high.

After years of bandwidth glut, capacity and demand were beginning to measure out. And, with upgrade costs prompting some of the early bandwidth players to give up once and for all, Cheyenne's STS technology, which would deliver information directly to homes and businesses through the water system, had a leapfrogging advantage. The promise remained intoxicating.

And Timmermans, Michelle, and Peter were getting rich, at least on paper. Timmermans was rich enough to buy a ncw Mercedes. Michelle was rich enough to purchase new houses for her parents and her sister, who had never gotten her act together. Peter was rich enough to buy whatever he wanted, and yet he couldn't decide what he wanted, so he bought season tickcts to FC Groningen games for most of his friends. In European technology circles, Peter had become a bit of a tech deity, showering his insights on younger adherents the way guys his age had done in the States in the late '90s. At work, he would show up at 10:30 in the morning, brainstorm a bit with the programmers, play a couple games of foosball, and leave by 4:30. Occasionally he'd make a speech to some technology crowd.

Life was good. Peter looked on with particular amusement as the press stumbled over itself for a chance to tell the rags to riches story of a new technology upstart and the men behind it, warts and all. It was a curious thing, Peter thought, how perfectly mundane conversations within Cheyenne could take on legendary proportions in the hands of journalists. He'd always thought Jesse James and Wyatt Earp were probably just normal guys behind the hyperbolic myths that reporters had created around them. Now he knew for certain that they were just everyday guys.

Everything Cheyenne did seemed to have a superlative attached to it now—"Game-changing," "Never Before," "Europe's Turn," "The New Tech Savior." Some of it was plain fiction. A Dutch newspaper ran an account of him in a supposed closed-door meeting with Timmermans discussing rollout phases of Cheyenne's technology. According to the article, Peter started swearing wildly at Timmermans, finally putting his fist into one of the pictures hanging on Timmermans' wall. Timmermans didn't have any pictures on his walls.

The International Herald Tribune called Peter the "the black-clad, side-burned, hell-raising king of all Euro geeks."

"Really?" he said to himself as he read the line in the folded paper from the comfort of his toilet. They said that in addition to being the technical brains behind Cheyenne, he was Europe's Marc Andreessen—a poster child of sorts for the continent's nerds who desperately wanted to take the tech baton from their American brethren. And like Andreessen, the press heaped a pitying praise on him as the wunderkind who got relegated to the sidelines while the suits and spin doctors maneuvered their way into the limelight.

Cheyenne was only a year and a half old, but already Peter knew it would be a short-term adventure. There would be a hangover at some point, and he didn't want to be around for it. For now, though, the money was good, and the prospects for even more were high.

Meanwhile, Vaughn had traveled over to Amsterdam to speak with the Cheyenne team. Behind closed doors at the party in Utah, Aaron had instructed him to put some golden handcuffs on them just in case any of them were getting antsy with their newfound success. Vaughn had already spent the morning with Timmermans and Michelle. Now he was about to meet with Peter.

Peter's office phone rang. "Peter, Mr. Vaughn asked if he could see you. Is it a good time?"

"I thought he was catching a plane back to the States." "He asked if he could have a final word before he left." "Let him in."

Vaughn ducked as he passed through the door to Peter's office. He was a giant, tall and slim. He had that salt and pepper hair that seemed to be congenital in successful businessmen's DNA. And his baritone voice—Peter couldn't help himself from being hypnotized by it. Shit, the man even smelled good.

"Peter. I wanted to swing by before I left."

"That was good of you."

Vaughn knew what he had to do. "Listen, Peter, I was just talking to Timmermans and Michelle about how well the whole announcement went, and how glad we are that all of you have been able to put some cash in the bank. I know that as someone coming from graduate school life it must seem like an awful lot of money."

"It does."

"It seems like that now, but a couple of years from now, it will seem natural, even normal. That's how money works. You'll want more things, more toys."

"Maybe."

"You will, believe me. Anyway, this financial stuff may seem complicated, but that all depends on the light in which you view it. It only *seems* complicated. I'm sure if you tried to explain the technology behind Cheyenne to me; I would feel the same way."

"Most basic thing in the world: water."

"Yes, but what you're setting out to do with it is hardly basic. You're creating the future, Peter, and that's gotta feel good."

"It's not a bad perk."

"No, it's not. There are other perks available to you, you know."

"Like what?"

"Well, the life blood of investment banking is relationships, preferably long-term relationships, like what we're doing with Cheyenne, for example. There are a lot of outfits out there that just churn clients, make the quick buck, and move on. Teestone is not like that."

"Really?" Peter said, somewhat sarcastically.

"Not at all. You see, Peter, my first priority is to make sure that the management teams of my clients are happy. Without happy management, it's just a house of cards waiting for a stiff wind to roll up."

"Ah huh."

"Now, some banks are bigger than Teestone. Some claim to have underwritten more deals in this sector. Some know Europe better than we do, but you guys put your faith in Teestone, and for that we are grateful."

"I'm just the tech guy."

"But without you, Peter, this whole thing would have been just another idea scribbled on a piece of paper."

"I'm glad you see it that way."

"I do, and here's what I want to do, Peter. I'll get our brokerage guys to open an account for you with Teestone. You could put $1 in it to get started if you want, or you could put $10,000, it's up to you."

"What sort of account?"

"A special account, the kind that we only do for top clients. We used to do it in the '90s. I've always thought it was something we should dust off and bring back. It's a way to show our appreciation. I won't bore you with the details, but it's tied to the IPO market. You see, Peter, there are dozens of other companies out there like Cheyenne with

117

real vision, and thankfully, they are starting to hit the market again. They need to raise money. You're lucky that you don't have to do that. You've got Cannondale bankrolling you now."

"If you consider that a bonus."

"It is. Believe me, you should feel good about the fact that you don't need to whore around to raise capital. It's been a tough few years. We only take on companies that we think are the real deal. I like to think of them as one big family of like-minded companies with like-minded management who want to change the world and do a little good. Cheyenne is in that league, Peter. You guys are Varsity. You get better jerseys."

"Is that right."

"Let me give you a better jersey, Peter. May I open this account for you? My people will take care of everything. You won't have to worry about a thing."

"I don't have to watch over it? Because I really don't have the time."

"No. We'll hook you up with a money manager who will do it for you. I think you'll be pleased by what you see."

Peter thought for a moment. "Have you made the same offer to Timmermans and Michelle?"

"Of course."

"And they took it?"

"Of course."

Suddenly, Peter had a vision of a winding river cutting

through the mountains of northern Wyoming, a river flush with browns and rainbow. The kind of money that was talking about could put him over the top, to a place where he wanted to be. But then again, he already had a lot of money, at least on paper. What Vaughn was describing seemed a bit too easy."

"I'll pass."

"You'll pass? What do you mean you'll pass?" Vaughn said, startled. "Do you realize, Peter, that these bubbles only come around every decade or so? Who knows what the next one will be—biotech, carbon trading, mortgages?"

"I guess I'll wait for the next bubble then."

"It won't be bandwidth and it won't be water, I'll tell you that right now. And that's what you do, Peter. You need to strike now before someone decides to come in and regulate this stuff."

"Look, Timmermans and Michelle can do what they want. That's their prerogative, but I'm going to pass."

"But why? It could mean a lot of money."

"I already have a lot of money."

"That's true, but wouldn't more be nice?"

"Possibly."

Vaughn was irritated. Aaron had sent him to Amsterdam to slap the kid around with dollar bills, and now the kid wasn't playing ball.

"Timmermans and Michelle will be surprised. Cannondale will be surprised. He doesn't want there to be ill will between the three of you. He wants to make sure that you guys share in the glory of what you're creating here."

"That's generous for a guy who has never set foot in this office."

"He's a busy man."

"Yeah, very busy."

"Look, I don't have time for this, Peter. The offer is on the table. Do you want it?"

Peter stared at Vaughn for a moment. He suspected it could amount to a lot of money.

"No."

"Suit yourself," Vaughn said, getting up out of the chair. "Mistake, big mistake."

Vaughn took a quick survey of Peter's office and shook his head. It was certainly a departure from Timmermans'. A large poster of FC Groningen's 2005 squad dominated one wall. A blue lava lamp oozed in the corner just beneath a velvet painting of Princess Diana. There was a small set of bull horns that Peter had won at a fair, and a naked female mannequin with a man's toupee glued where her pubic hair should have been.

"Nice toupee," Vaughn said.

"Thanks. Give my best to Cannondale."

Chapter 20

Hayden was in a cab heading to his apartment in New York when his Blackberry started chirping.

"Hello."

"Hayden?"

"This is Hayden. Who's this?"

"It's Michelle—Michelle Vandermullen."

Hayden paused for a moment. *Michelle from Cheyenne?* She sounded like she had been crying.

"Michelle, what is it? What's wrong?"

"I'm in New York. Can we meet?"

"Of course. Where?"

"The Oak Room at the Plaza."

"Give me 30 minutes."

What was Michelle doing in New York? Did she come over with Timmermans? Was Aaron in town? He'd soon find out.

He spotted her in the back of the bar in one of the comfortable leather chairs at a table for two. She was nursing a martini—straight up, olives. It was just one more thing Hayden liked about her.

"Michelle."

She smiled a worried smile and motioned for Hayden to sit down.

A waiter came over. "Drink, sir?"

"Bourbon and ginger."

"Michelle, what are you doing in New York? Is

Timmermans here? Aaron?"

"No, neither of them. I had to get away, Hayden."

"Away from what?"

"Cheyenne, Timmermans, Peter, Aaron—the whole thing. It's …"

"It's what?"

"It's all-consuming. It's all I work on. I needed a holiday. I needed to be anonymous."

"New York's a good place for that, unless you're famous," Hayden said, trying to make a joke. Michelle flashed a half-hearted smile, as if to say "nice try." She was so damn pretty—thin, but not too thin; great shoulders, long neck. The way she ate the olives was borderline erotic.

"Things are going well at Cheyenne, no?" Hayden asked, trying to keep the conversation going.

"Too well."

"What do you mean?"

"We're making a lot of money, Hayden. A lot of money."

"What's wrong with that?"

"Nothing, in principle."

"Then what's the issue?"

"What is it that you say … 'the ends don't always justify the means'?"

"That's right. Which means are you talking about?"

"I don't know. It's just the way that … well …"

It was a chore pulling information out of her.

"How well do you know Aaron, Hayden?"

"At this point, probably as well as anyone knows him. Why?"

"No, I mean, do you really feel that you know him?"

"Aaron has always been a bit of a puzzle. I think anyone who knows him would tell you that."

"I'm under a lot of pressure to make the numbers look good, Hayden. More than I've ever felt."

"Pressure from whom?"

"It doesn't matter. I've gotten creative before, but not like this."

"What do you mean, Michelle?"

"It doesn't matter."

"Yes it does, Michelle. Tell me. I want to know."

"It's better that you don't know, Hayden."

"Why? Are you in some sort of trouble?"

"No. They…"

"Who is 'they'? Tell me, Michelle. Who are you talking about?"

"I can't, Hayden. I can't!" She banged her fist on the table and started to cry.

"Ok, ok, Michelle. That's fine. I didn't mean to upset you."

"Can we leave? Can we get some air? I need some air."

"Of course."

Hayden opened his wallet and left cash. Michelle took her belongings. They exited onto 59th Street and crossed traffic to the sidewalk along Central Park. A hansom cab was parked there. The horse had his nose in a feed bag.

"Purfect night for a ride now, isn't it?" the Irish driver said. "Where can I take yous?"

Michelle stroked the horse's head gently, oblivious to the driver's question.

"$45, once around the park. What de yous say?"

Hayden shook his head as if to say "she's not in the mood." The man got it.

Hayden put his arm around Michelle to move her along. They walked the wall of the park, making their way to Columbus Circle.

"Hayden. Can we just sit here on the wall?"

"Sure."

"I mean, just sit. No words. No questions?"

"Of course."

Michelle struggled to smile. A taxi blared. A kid on a skateboard rode past on the sidewalk stones. Tail lights flickered.

"Thank you, Hayden," she said. She touched the side of his face the same way she had stroked the horse. Then she kissed him.

Part III
Chapter 21
(2006)

For Immediate Release:

European Commission Continues Review of Cheyenne Acquisition

Amsterdam, The Netherlands and Salt Lake City, Utah—March 16, 2006: Cheyenne B.V. today received notice that the European Commission continues to review the pending sale of the company to Lyrical, Inc.

Cheyenne remains confident that the Commission will approve the transaction and that the sale will happen on schedule by the end of the year.

Cheyenne and Lyrical look forward to their continuing discussions with the European Commission to demonstrate the competitive benefits that the acquisition will deliver.

Last year, Cheyenne announced that it had agreed to be purchased by Lyrical, Inc. for US $300 million. For more information go to http://www.cheyenne-acquisition.com

* * * *

Graham Eatwell tossed the press release in the trash. "American PR stunt," he grumbled.

Cannondale's people were trying to turn up the heat by cranking out press releases intimating that the Commission was likely to approve the acquisition. But that kind of tactic was not going to work on Eatwell. He'd decide on the acquisition when he was good and ready, and no bloody Yank was going to rush him.

The sun hadn't shone in Brussels for 28 days. The city's trench-coated inhabitants scurried from building to building on stone pavements under black umbrellas in an animated version of a Magritte canvas. Sometimes the stones would shift when stepped on and spit out a stream of water the way oysters do when they jettison waste.

That's it, Brussels is one big oyster bed, Eatwell thought to himself as he hurried down Rue Franklin, happy to have finally found an analogy for a thought he'd had for a while.

He was going to have lunch at La Trattoria, one of the many Italian places decorated in hardwood and amateur wall murals that surrounded the Berlaymont building, home of the European Commission. The Berlaymont had finally shed the enormous white sheet that had shrouded it for more than a decade like some Christo exhibit, part of a project to eviscerate asbestos from the bowels of the building.

Eatwell had summoned Kuipers to eat with him. Funny, he thought, when they were boys they were all about cricket bats and rugby balls. Now it was all so serious. Eatwell had made a career of diplomacy, which in his mind was nothing more than a license to fib for one's country, to defend it at all costs, whoever the aggressor. In his case, his borders went well beyond the White Cliffs of Dover. He was odd for a Brit. His nation was Europe, and even though affected sophistication wouldn't allow him to gush patriotism, he was, at heart, the soppiest of flag wavers.

Kuipers was already at the table.

"Graham," Kuipers said, standing up for the embrace.

"Menno," Eatwell said, hugging and looking Kuipers in the eye for an extended moment. "It's tremendous to see you. What has it been, six months? Please, sit."

"So, your star keeps rising, huh Graham?"

"Hardly."

"Enjoy it. The kind of success you've been having doesn't come around all that often."

"Enough of me, Menno. How are you?"

"I'm well. I'm planning to retire next year."

"You're not? I thought you'd work until they carted you out of the office."

"I'm bored, Graham. There are few challenges left for me. I had a privileged childhood, lived through the war, met my wifc, buried my wife. I don't feel the need to prove anything to anyone anymore."

"I'm still saddened when I think about your Karin. How long has it been now, six years?"

"Yes, six. It's just that I find it difficult to get excited about much of anything anymore, Graham, save our new mutual friend."

"Cannondale?"

"Yes."

"What's the situation?"

"He's got lobbyists coming to see me, Graham."

"Me, too. Relentless. And these bloody press releases."

"So you understand what I mean. The whole thing is

127

beginning to get out of hand. I wish I had fully understood it earlier—the technology, I mean. I can't help feeling responsible for allowing this thing to get into motion."

A waiter arrived. Kuipers ordered wild boar soup as a starter, followed by Ossobuco. Eatwell ordered a caprese salad and sole meunière. They asked for a bottle of white Sancerre.

"Well, there's no need to flog it to death, Menno. What's done is done, and whatever progress has been made to date has no bearing on the acquisition proceedings."

"You're not going to let it through, are you Graham?"

"Of course not. I never had any intention of letting it through, but I can't give that impression. I'm supposed to be steeped in objectivity, don't you know."

"Graham, I haven't felt so against something in quite some time."

"That makes two of us."

"I feel like you and I are the only ones minding the store on this one, Graham. No one else seems to care about Cannondale. I can't let it happen."

"Then don't."

"But I'm getting pressure from a lot of directions on this. I've got U.S. congressmen calling my office, and I've got bloody German and Dutch members of the European Parliament doing Cannondale's bidding for him. Last week, I got a rather odd, but polite letter from Riga-Tech, the Russian company that sold the satellite to Cheyenne. I've got the U.S. Trade Representative coming over next week threatening retaliation if we don't maintain openness in the technology sector. Bloody U.S. Trade Representative is coming over here in the name of free trade. Can you believe that? It's as if Cannondale has his own personal battering ram."

The starters arrived. "*Bon appetit*," said the waiter. "By the way, what did the letter say?" asked Eatwell.

"Which letter ... oh, from the Russians—Riga-Tech? It asked for clarification on our current stance. Reading between the lines, I take it they don't get paid in full by Cannondale for their satellite until it goes up."

"What is your current stance—public I mean?"

"I don't know. It's going to be tricky. There's no real legal basis for denying Cheyenne clearance to use satellites and send signals within the Netherlands as part of its network. For Christ's sake, Graham, Cannondale seems to have even gotten to the prime minister."

"DeWeld?"

"Yes. He's a big Cheyenne fan these days. Thinks it's great for competition. Thinks it's great for the Netherlands and for Barroso's Lisbon Agenda to promote economic growth and innovation throughout Europe. He wants to be the technological savior of the Netherlands before the next election. And he's been spending a lot of time in Silicon Valley. I think he wishes he was part of all that. Scotland's got Silicon Glen, England's got Silicon Fen, DeWeld is looking to create his own little Silicon Canal."

"Your prime minister doesn't have the spine to stop

this, Menno. But you do, *and* you've got the platform. You've got to get creative, Menno. You're going to get steamrolled if you're not careful. But you can't come across as a zealot on this."

"What do you suggest?"

"I don't know."

Kuipers and Eatwell ate and talked. Waiters dashed in and out of the kitchen. The hostess took a reservation on the phone. "*Oui monsieur*," she said. "*Á treize heures et demi. Pas de problème.*"

Chapter 22

"I hate Frankfurt," Timmermans said from a comfortable chair across from Hayden in the lobby of the airport hotel. "Not a damn thing to do here."

Aaron had given a speech earlier in the day at a gathering of bankers, and then immediately boarded his plane for the return to Utah. Aaron had asked Hayden to stay behind to be a fly on the wall during Timmermans' meeting with the two men who ran the Russian satellite company, Riga-Tech. The point of the meeting was to keep up relations with the Russians. Aaron had only forked over half the money to purchase the satellite, with the agreement that the other half would come upon launch. He knew the Russians were getting antsy with the regulatory circus.

It was vintage Aaron, having a man stay to observe and eventually report. Aaron knew that at some point down the road, in a quiet moment when it was just the two of them over a glass of Pinot Noir at Kshanti, he could turn to Hayden and say, "So, how was Frankfurt, my friend?"

"Funny how Aaron seems to disappear just when things are getting interesting, don't you think?" Timmermans said, digging for the silver cigarette case in his coat pocket.

"What's the situation with Riga-Tech?" asked Hayden.

"I'm the bishop and you're the rook, that's the situation. It's all part of one big chess game, my friend, and the guy who's moving the pieces is about 35,000 feet over

Newfoundland right about now."

Hayden took his micro-recorder from his sport coat pocket and clicked it on. "Note to self: what am I doing here?"

Two men walked into the room. Hayden had an immediate flashback to a series of advertisements that used to run on the Metro North trains out of New York's Grand Central Station. They were called "The Rothman's Man," and were a collection of WPA-style images of square-jawed men clad in Rothman's suits scaling buildings, pulling trees out of the ground with their bare hands, or pumping hand cars down railroad tracks with their ties flapping in the wind. Hayden vaguely remembered the tag lines said things along the lines of "Adores his in-laws, passed on Mensa, and really enjoys his commute."

The figures now standing in front of Hayden were the Russian version of Rothman men. They were life-sized placards of the new Russian economy—suits, slicked back hair, tough, humorless. It was interesting to actually see them in person. Hayden had become curious when Aaron asked him to stay behind for the meeting and did a little homework.

The first man was Zlotnikov. He was young and well built. The second man was Tebelis. He had dark glasses and a turtleneck sweater, the kind of garb that could have snatched him a role as one of the mute, East German bad guys in a Bond film. Both men had firm handshakes, Zlotnikov, in particular. Neither man smiled. It was a funny scene; one Hayden would have ridiculed as "B" movie stuff had he not been a real-life participant. He had a hard time taking it seriously. The most intriguing bit of all, though, was that the two men weren't what they said they were. On paper, they ran Riga-Tech. The reality according to Hayden's contacts, however, was that Tebelis owned nightclubs, and Zlotnikov dealt in stolen Mercedes. Hayden hadn't shared these factoids with anyone.

"Who's he?" Zlotnikov asked Timmermans, pointing to Hayden. "This is Hayden Campbell, Cannondale's Director of Communications."

"Director of Communications of what?"

"Good question," Hayden said.

"Cannondale asked him to be here," Timmermans interjected, trying to keep things moving.

They made their way into a quiet anteroom. It could have been any business hotel, anywhere. The idea was to fly in, take care of affairs, wash down a wurst with a glass of Spaten, and fly out again.

"This Dutch man, Kuipers, he does not like us," Zlotnikov began. "We have good satellites; you have good technology, no?"

"It's not you he has the problem with, it's Cannondale," said Timmermans, lighting a Dunhill.

"He does not want to take American money? Idiot."

"They want to keep the technology in European hands."

"And you? Are *you* not European?"

Timmermans looked puzzled.

"It does not bother you?" Zlotnikov asked.

"I'm a businessman."

"I see," Zlotnikov said, pleased by Timmermans' candor. He took a handkerchief out and wiped his brow. The man didn't appear the least bit nervous, but he was a world-class sweater.

"We want to be in a position to launch the satellite when Kuipers and his Euro-cronies lose their little battle," Timmermans said.

"Are you so confident that he will lose his battle?" Zlotnikov said, scratching his pug nose.

"This is larger than one jingoistic bureaucrat," Timmermans said, mashing his cigarette into the ashtray.

"We know something of bureaucrats," Tebilis grunted.

They were the first words Timmermans and Hayden had heard the man speak. Hayden watched quietly as the men completed their business by toasting the universal thread of capitalism with raised vodka glasses and a bowl of caviar.

With the deal completed, Zlotnikov began to talk about the "New Russia" under Putin. Hayden's sources indicated that Zlotnikov and Tebelis were both actually Latvian by origin, but grew up in Moscow. Zlotnikov was sixteen when Yuri Vladmirovich Andropov became General Secretary of the Soviet Union. Zlotnikov's parents sent him to school to study engineering, which led to his interest in technology. "This Andropov, he was a poet as well as an overfed bureaucrat you know," Zlotnikov said sarcastically, bumping back more shots of vodka. He was getting increasingly drunk.

"Andropov?" asked Hayden, trying to imagine the irony.

"Yes. He thought writers should be given the freedom to help the party and the state in its struggle for order. I remember one of his pathetic poems published after his death. It was called ... let's see ... 'Power Corrupts.'"

"Let's hear it then," Hayden said.

Zlotnikov stood up, paused dramatically and then recited the poem, word for word. When he finished, he bowed and said "translates better in Russian. I give you Y.V. Andropov, my friends, poet extraordinaire, and an idiot for sure."

The men clapped wildly, laughing. Hayden was beginning to like Zlotnikov. Just then, several unescorted women, a mixture of Germans and Hungarians, entered the room—an arrangement, no doubt, made by Zlotnikov and Tebelis. It was Hayden's cue to leave. He didn't want to get too chummy with these guys. One deep stare into the eyes of the Hungarian girl in his lap and he would be contemplating a lifelong relationship with her that would end three weeks later. That's the way it was with him. Besides, Michelle was on his mind.

Hayden smiled at the absurdity of four strange women entering a room to sit in the laps of men they didn't know. What if people did that on the street or on the bus, or at the opera? Maybe the world would be a very different place, free of inhibitions like actually knowing someone before you slept with them. Maybe it was already that way. Maybe *knowing* people didn't really matter anymore. Knowing someone didn't stop people from mistreating each other. Having tea together didn't stave off deceit. A lifetime of beers and baseball games together at the local bar didn't stop men from sleeping with their best friends' wives. What was the point in *knowing*?

Hayden looked over at Timmermans, who was enjoying himself with two of the ladies. They were messing up his hair and loosening his tie. Timmermans had a broad smile on his face, the kind an awkward prep school boy would have on a visit to a brothel.

Chapter 23

Timmermans had read somewhere that in every two miles the average driver makes four hundred observations, forty decisions, and one mistake. Once every five hundred miles, one of those mistakes leads to a near collision, and once every sixty-one thousand miles one of those mistakes leads to a crash.

Timmermans had just crashed. Her name was Malene. She came from Bavaria. She had large breasts.

He looked at the clock on the nightstand. "*Grote ver Jezus!*" he shouted. His plane was leaving in just over an hour. Malene's artificially-tanned forearm lay across his hairy chest.

"Wake up," he said, stirring her.

"Eh?" she said in a morning stupor. Timmermans got the sense that she was used to being awakened this way.

"We've ... you've ... got to go. I need to catch a plane."

The full impact of what had transpired began to hit him. His heart rate accelerated. He began to talk to himself as he scurried around the hotel room picking up bits of his belongings. "Going to be okay. Just a mistake," he said to himself. "Not something I regularly do. Love my wife. Can't believe this happened!"

He had compromised himself. Nothing he could do could change that. He picked up Malene's black lace underwear and tossed it on the bed.

Malene saw Timmermans look at his watch. "Yes, okay, I go," she said, making her way to the bathroom. Her body was beautiful. Ten hours ago it was the most beautiful thing he'd ever seen. He had pounced on it like some crazed animal. Now, although her body remained beautiful, he wanted to dispose of it.

He sat at the end of the bed. The bathroom door was open. "Tell me something. Why do men do this?" he said in a palliative attempt to make himself feel better.

"You want to talk of such things now?"

"No, you're right … I …"

"I suppose people want what they cannot have, and when they get it, they feel sad."

Timmermans thought for a moment, puzzled. He wasn't sure if what she had said was profound or pitiful.

"Call a cab for me," Malene said. "Go have lunch with your wife."

Chapter 24

"Good evening ladies and gentlemen, I'm Nigel Trickelbank. Tonight our broadcast of "Any Questions?" comes to you from the beautiful Palais Royal in Brussels. The topic: "Nation States in an Internet World." We're honored this evening to have Michel Lorraine, President of FranzCom, France's largest mobile operator; David Moore, Assistant U.S. Trade Representative for European Affairs; and Sir Graham Eatwell, European Competition Commissioner.

"Let's begin. The Internet is quite possibly the single most powerful threat to the nation state as we know it. Autocratic regimes fear its ability to expose corruption and tyranny, while democratic governments struggle to harness its power for collective good. The result is a borderless world where unilateral decisions are becoming increasingly rare. What is the landscape going to look like going forward? Who's in control? Who has lost control?

"Our first question from the audience tonight comes from Mrs. Susan Hale."

"Thank you. My question is this: Europeans are accustomed to seeing American companies get their way when it comes to international trade. In your opinion, is the Internet causing a shift in that balance of power?"

Moore

"Thank you for your question. I have to say, I disagree with the premise. More often than not, the United

States has not gotten its way in the trade arena. But that's history. Let's look at the situation as it stands right now. The backdrop to every conversation that Europeans and Americans are having at the moment—be it political, social or economic—is still Iraq. We are pleased that the fence-mending has begun and that Europe and the United States are working together to help Iraqis build better lives for themselves.

"This kind of partnership on global issues needs to carry over to our trade relationship. In order to keep the partnership thriving, we must recognize trade for what it is—a sensitive element of every country's sovereignty.

"Sometimes you lose, sometimes you win, and sometimes you have an extended stalemate. It always has been that way.

"Trade is being impacted by the Internet much in the same way that other areas of society are. It has added an element of speed by creating efficiencies, like the ability to double or triple inventory turns, or streamline supply chains and procurement systems in ways that were not possible even ten years ago. I think going forward what you're going to see are governments generally having to act more quickly. I'm sure Monsieur Lorraine can attest to that."

Lorraine

"Certainly. Companies, too. The Internet has introduced an element of competition that has forced every company—French, German, American—to

reassess what it really wants to be. Ten years ago, FranzCom offered just mobile phone service and paging. Now we offer text messaging, photos, email, streaming video, and wireless Internet access."

Trickelbank

"Interesting. Commissioner Eatwell, how are you finding the Internet affecting what you do at the Commission?"

Eatwell

"Not so surprisingly, it is making bureaucracies more accessible to everyday people. The Commission has a reputation, sometimes deserved, sometimes undeserved, of being an insular bastion of grey suits making closed-door decisions about the fate of Europe. The Internet has allowed us to become far more transparent with the roughly 460 million people who now make up the European Union. Economically, it allows people to immediately see data about their own country vis-a-vis other members of the EU. Linguistically, it allows us to simultaneously post versions of EU law in all official languages, rather than waiting for paper. Culturally, EU citizens have an easier time planning vacations, or monitoring cultural events throughout the EU. One of the goals of the EU has always been to be borderless. The Internet is a tool that is making that happen."

Trickelbank

"Thank you. Our next question comes from Mr. Philipe Wouters."

Wouters

*"My question is for Commissioner Eatwell.
Commissioner, you mentioned that the Commission has a
reputation of being a body of grey suits making decisions
about the fate of Europe."*

Eatwell

*"I said sometimes deservedly, and sometimes
undeservedly."*

Wouters

*"Yes, thank you. Sir, we've seen an increasing number
of mergers and acquisitions originating outside of Europe
that have been rejected by Brussels, particularly from your
office. In fact, you've earned a bit of a reputation for
taking a hard line with global mergers. I can imagine that
this is a new phenomenon for our trading partners. Is it
likely to cause friction going forward?"*

Eatwell

*"Thank you for asking that. Let me be very clear that
neither my office nor the Commission as a whole
approaches a potential merger or acquisition with any
bias. In many ways, we try to act like judges. We assess
the facts and then make a determination of what's best for
competition in Europe. That is our mandate—the interests
of Europe, not one or two particular countries, or one
company over another. When we see a situation where
one entity could end up with a dominant position in the
marketplace, it's our duty to address that. We're seeing a
lot of this, particularly in the technology sector where the*

United States often has a competitive advantage."

Trickelbank

"I'm sure Mr. Moore would probably like to add to that."

Moore

"I would, thank you. What the Commissioner says is true. Fair competition must be upheld, but the circumstances are not always black and white. Trade does not occur in a vacuum. The American government is always going to look at what's best for consumers as a whole, not only consumers in our country, but hopefully around the globe. When a situation arises where consumers can benefit from a proposed merger, it's our opinion that a body such as the Commission must take that into account."

Trickelbank

"But what Commissioner Eatwell says about American technology has merit, does it not?"

Moore

"I'm not sure that it does. It makes the assumption that American technology is always superior to European technology, which we know is not the case. I think it's folly to assume that an American technology always has a head start. Yes, on most days, capital is more readily available in Silicon Valley than it is in, say, Silicon Glen, but this shouldn't really be a factor in the Commission's mind. Consumers today have accumulated a body of rights. Many of those rights center around getting technologies into their hands

regardless of where the technologies originate, regardless of who is footing the bill, and regardless of who is making a profit. To deny consumers progressive technology is to stifle. And to stifle is to limit the kind of progress I think we all want to see."

Trickelbank

"I can't help but make the connection between your comments and the current acquisition being reviewed by the Commission involving Cheyenne, B.V."

Moore

"I don't think it's productive to get into specific cases. Suffice it to say that consumers are in the driver's seat these days. To deny them what they crave does no one much good."

Trickelbank

"Commissioner Eatwell?"

Eatwell

"I agree. This isn't the venue to get into specific cases, but I will emphasize once again that while the desires of consumers must be of paramount concern, they are not the only ingredient involved with making a merger decision. If a case arises where one group is primed to take a dominant position, we must look at that carefully, and then act."

"Shithead," Pettigrew erupted as he listened to Eatwell's remarks on a radio in Aaron's room at the Hotel Amigo in Brussels. Aaron sat next to him. Hayden was busy at a table in the corner cranking on a speech.

"He might as well tell the world that he's not going to

let this thing go through," Pettigrew said.

"Looks that way, doesn't it," Aaron said, sipping a cup of coffee. "The Belgians do a good cup of coffee, don't they. It's Brazilian, you know."

"What's Brazilian?"

"The beans—the beans that they use to make the coffee. That's why European coffee tastes better than American coffee. The Euros use Brazilian coffee beans. We use crap from Honduras and Tanzania."

"Damn the coffee, Aaron. Are you listening to what's going on here?"

"Relax, Elliot. That's *your* job."

"I know. That's why it's givin' me a knot in my stomach. Aaron, you've gotta address this in your speech tomorrow at the American Chamber of Commerce. You can't let this lie."

"I don't intend to, but dropping this into a speech is just going to fuel the flames. I'm the last person who should be commenting on this."

"Agreed," Hayden said from the corner.

"Excuse me, but why the hell are you here?" Pettigrew said to Hayden, annoyed.

"Because I invited him," Aaron said sternly. "Because he's the guy who puts my words on paper. Because he's the Director of Communications. Got it?"

"Director of what?" Pettigrew said, incredulous.

"Communications," Hayden said, shrugging his shoulders comically. It had become a bit of a running joke. That said,

Hayden was taken aback by the compliment that Aaron had just paid him. Aaron was, of course, his own action agent, the final arbiter of what he said and did not say, but it was flattering to think that Aaron had come to think so highly of him. Plus, Pettigrew had been put in his place.

"What do you want to do then, Aaron?" Pettigrew asked.

"I want you to pay another visit to the Water Miser."

"Kuipers?"

"Yep."

Chapter 25

Eatwell caught the phone in his living room on the third ring.

"Graham. It's Menno."

"Menno. How the devil are you?"

"Not well, Graham."

"What is it?"

"I received a call from DeWeld yesterday. He caught your performance on "Any Questions?""

"Your prime minister must have some time on his hands. I didn't know he was a fan of mine."

"He's not, Graham, at least not these days. He expressed concern that you seem to have already made your decision about Cheyenne, Graham. From the tone of your comments, I can't disagree with him."

"Was I that transparent?"

"A bit. Graham, it may be better if you refrain from making any public comments at the moment. I'm getting pressure here."

"From whom?"

"It doesn't matter."

Eatwell could hear an ambulance siren in the background. "Menno, where are you?"

"At a pay phone. Someone tapped my office phone."

"That's not cricket, now is it?"

"Graham, listen. Just please do me the favor of staying out of the limelight a bit. Can you do that?"

"If you're asking me to tone it down, yes, sure, Menno. What's going on, my friend?"

"Nothing. Graham, could you do me one other favor? I'd like you to make contact with a gentleman named Jagmetti in Zurich. He's a banker. He is the gentleman who helped Cheyenne get their hands on a satellite through that Russian company, Riga-Tech."

"Why do I need to contact him?"

"Because he's the kind of man that fixes things, Graham. I think he could be helpful to us. I've already spoken to him. His number is 411 311 6414. Have you got that?"

"… 6414. Got it. This is a strange request, Menno."

"That doesn't matter now, Graham. Jagmetti will explain. Just promise me that you'll get in touch with him. He's expecting your call."

"I'll call him. Don't worry. Just take care of yourself."

"I've got to go, Graham. I'll call you next week."

Eatwell hung up the phone, thought for a moment, reached for his cup of Earl Grey from the coffee table, and took a sip. Derek walked into the room dressed in a white bathrobe. He was younger than Eatwell—somewhere in his early 40s. He had brown hair and a wind-burned face from the documentary shoot he had just completed in Botswana. It was Sunday, the day they normally slept in, read papers, and kept the rest of the world at a distance. Derek could see the concerned look on Eatwell's face.

"What is it?"

"Nothing," Eatwell said, opening his arms. Derek went to him. They hugged. It was the kind of comfort that Graham could never allow himself to either give or receive from a woman. Even so, it always seemed temporary. That's the way it was with them, some weeks together, other weeks on their own. It had to work that way, at least for Eatwell's benefit. Being deep in the closet was a necessity in Graham's world. He didn't really even view himself as gay, at least in terms of making a formal statement. It seemed so final. To him, his sexuality was like having dual citizenship—he had the freedom to come and go; he just tended to prefer one place over another.

Eatwell sat down in his leather winged chair. Derek rifled through the newspaper.

"I think I'll go to Amsterdam next week," Eatwell announced.

"Amsterdam. Why?"

"To see Menno."

"I see. How's his head?"

"What do you mean?"

"Menno's head. It's oddly-shaped, no?"

"What?"

"Don't you think so? Like an egg."

Eatwell shook his head. He hadn't really noticed the attributes of Menno's cranium, but the egg analogy held, in more ways than one. There was a sort of Humpty Dumpty fragility to Menno. It had been that way since their youth. It seemed that Eatwell was always looking out for Menno.

Chapter 26

Schiphol Airport on the outskirts of Amsterdam started early in the last century as a military base that consisted of a handful of barracks and a mud pool which served as a runway. It had since grown. So had the nearby Aalsmeer Flower Market. It is now the largest flower auction in the world.

Elliot Pettigrew had only been through Schiphol twice before. He liked it. It wasn't the kind of tat that you saw in American airports, particularly JFK, which to him was one of the more embarrassing welcome mats to any country.

Schiphol had the sophistication that one would expect in an international airport—leather chairs, restaurants, places to lie down, a hospital, TV rooms, reading rooms, crucial-looking women, tall girls, fat businessmen, huddled clans of Hasidim, Arabs, Africans dressed in fruit-colored robes, and beer and booze flowing 24 hours a day. It even had an animal hotel where God's creatures could eat, drink, and exercise while in transit. The place didn't have an off switch. It was the Times Square of airports.

Pettigrew took the train into the city. He opted to walk from Amsterdam Central Station in the direction of the Dam. It was only five o'clock in the evening, but the dark cloud hanging over the city made it seem later. Cars and motorcycles had their headlights on. The decision to meet with Kuipers had been a bit spontaneous. Neither man had mentioned it to anyone. Kuipers didn't want it getting around the ministry, and consequently out to the press.

Pettigrew had all he needed in his briefcase. He jumped on a tram. "Round Two," he thought to himself as the car glided through the city. He vowed not to be quite as diplomatic with Kuipers this time around. In the briefcase was a strongly-worded letter from the U.S. Trade Representative to Dutch Prime Minister DeWeld indicating that if the Ministry of Waterworks did not come forth with a valid rationale for why a company like Cheyenne, which was using European technology, couldn't receive satellite rights—something that the Ministry had originally indicated it was partial to—there would be hell to pay when it came to U.S.-Dutch relations.

It was the bombshell Pettigrew needed to transform Kuipers from pencil-necked bureaucrat with a Napoleon complex into a helpless jellyfish, and he was relishing it. The letter would put DeWeld in a tough position. He had been pulling some strings to get his eldest daughter into the University of Chicago's MBA program, a program that by all accounts would not accept her based on her academic qualifications. He also had an upcoming election in 18 months.

DeWeld had always had an excellent relationship with the U.S. Through his stewardship, he had been able to carve out a nice slice of the American technology boom for the Netherlands via a series of tax breaks for U.S. companies and technology alliances between American and Dutch research facilities. In many ways, Cheyenne was a poster child for 21st-century transatlantic collaboration. There was no way that DeWeld was going to let an aging minister like Kuipers with less than two years until retirement—a guy that by all accounts DeWeld didn't like anyway—mess that up.

Pettigrew climbed down from the tram in front of Kuipers' building. He could see the light on in the second-floor office.

Kuipers lit a cigarette at his desk. The smoke slithered upwards into the bluish halogen beam as he waited for the American with the strange Louisiana accent. Even without knowing about the letter in Pettigrew's briefcase, Kuipers had come to a conclusion. He hoped Graham would understand. It ate him up, the realization that the Americans—and Cannondale in particular—might get their way. Kuipers didn't dislike Americans. On the contrary, he quite liked their optimism. But he didn't like losing to them, or anyone for that matter. He planned to inform Pettigrew that he had decided to grant Cheyenne full satellite rights. He had already informed his prime minister, who expressed his support.

Once he had made up his mind, it felt as if an anvil had been lifted off his chest. He was getting too old for this kind of political chess anyway. In less than 24 months, he would retire to his house in Spain. His grandchildren would visit. He would take long walks and re-read the great philosophers.

The doorbell rang. Kuipers had let his secretary go

early that evening. He got up and walked to her desk to hit the button that opened the downstairs door. Pettigrew paused a few seconds. He looked at his briefcase and realized that he wanted to have the letter in the breast pocket of his coat for easy access. He figured gunslingers didn't carry their weapons in a Samsonite, so why should he? He set the briefcase on the ground and opened it. A stiff gust reached in and yanked the letter out, blowing it down the sidewalk.

"Judas Priest," Pettigrew called out, chasing the letter. Another gust lifted it into the air and launched it in front of the building next door. He grabbed it as it floated to the ground.

Just then, a deafening explosion ripped through the first floor of Kuipers' building, followed immediately by a second blast. The force hurled Pettigrew's body into the street, depositing him like a piece of luggage that had fallen off a truck.

Black smoke billowed out of the building. Glass lay strewn in the street. A car alarm shrieked like a startled bird warning other members of the animal kingdom of danger.

Chapter 27

This TV is crap, Peter thought to himself as he ate a bowl of corn flakes and watched his team, FC Groningen, beat up Utrecht on the screen.

Sirens blared outside his window in a Doppler effect. His Blackberry danced on the glass surface of the coffee table.

"Ah, hell," he said, looking at the number. It was Timmermans. Peter ignored it and went back to watching the game. The Blackberry went off a second time.

Timmermans, again. This time, Peter replied. "What do you need?"

"Turn on the news, Peter."

"I'm watching the game."

"Just turn it on, Peter."

Peter flicked channels. He watched as images of twisted metal and rubble flashed before him. An excited reporter explained what had happened. People were dead. One of them was Minister Menno Kuipers. The police were at a loss as to who would want to blow up the building.

"Jesus," Peter said. "What the hell is going on?"

"I'm not sure."

"This just happen?"

"About 40 minutes ago."

"Cannondale …" Peter said softly.

"What's that, Peter?"

"Ah, nothing. I was just saying, ah … does

Cannondale …"

"Does Cannondale what?"

"Does he know about this?"

"He'll know soon enough. I don't know where he is. He's not answering his cell phone."

"This is bizarre," Peter said.

"Apparently Pettigrew was there."

"In the building? What was he doing there?"

"I don't know."

* * * *

Several hours away by car, in Brussels, Graham Eatwell had opened the window in his den. It was an unusually warm night in Brussels for early March. He was reading Thomas More's *Utopia* when he heard a car pull up on the street in front of his apartment. The engine went silent. Eatwell was having a hard time concentrating on the book and increasingly became fixated on the presence of the car.

He hadn't heard the doors open or close. Funny, he thought to himself, how we are conditioned to expect a certain course of action—a car parks on a street, engine goes off, doors are supposed to open, then close, maybe there's some laughter, maybe a conversation. When the course of action doesn't happen the way that we expect, we become curious.

Eatwell waited to hear the car doors. Nothing. He tried hard to focus on the page he was reading, but he couldn't. He had to take a look outside. He rose from his chair and moved to the window where he gently peered from behind the curtain. It was a black car, or maybe dark blue. The lights were off. He couldn't see anybody, but certainly there had to be someone. As his eyes adjusted he could make out one head in the car, then two. He couldn't see any facial features, but he had the feeling that the two orbs were looking in his direction. He backed away from the curtain.

He'd never seen the car before. Probably just a couple having a conversation or a fight before they got out and walked along the sidewalk. But they weren't leaving. They just hung around, looking in the direction of his townhouse.

Eatwell laid the book down on a side table. It was deadly quiet; it had been that way for the past several hours. He wanted some background noise. He picked up the remote and turned on the TV news. What he saw and heard next took the wind out of him.

* * * *

Hayden was in his apartment in New York. He had just made himself a bourbon & ginger and turned on a jazz CD by a new kid named Jacky Terrasson. As he began to take off his shirt for a shower, he looked out of the window onto the Park Slope section of Brooklyn, his home for the past four years. The sun was dropping. A group of girls played hopscotch on a homemade sidewalk outline. Farther down, two women in peach-colored dresses chatted. One had a grocery bag overflowing with papayas and mangoes. He liked the vitality of the place.

The phone rang.

"Hayden, it's Benbow. Turn on your TV."

Chapter 28

It was the call that Hayden had half anticipated since he began working for Cannondale. Benbow—CIA crew chief, former Navy intelligence, Vietnam vet, career curmudgeon, and Hayden's former boss.

Hayden's Arabic language training and his technology skills meant that the Langley boys had him on their speed dials. Once upon a time, he had been one of their budding stars. Benbow had taken a shine to him in a way that he had toward no other neophyte, that is, at least until the day Hayden walked away from it, tired, pissed off, worn down by the bureaucracy.

When he formally left the Agency, they negotiated that he would occasionally be called upon for assistance. Now was such a time. The master/student relationship between Benbow and Hayden had died a while ago, but the kid was talented. The Agency needed Hayden, and Hayden had a soft spot for helping it. Notch it up to duty or intrigue, Hayden didn't really know which, but when Benbow called, he usually responded.

Benbow's way of punishing Hayden was through periodic calls like this one, when Hayden found himself working for someone who raised suspicion. Benbow had some vague intel on Cannondale. Besides, Cannondale was the world's sixth richest man, which in Benbow's book made him worthy of suspicion, if not jealousy.

"I thought we were through after your last 'Dear John'

letter, Benbow," Hayden said with a laugh, moving the phone from one ear to the other.

"You've been hanging around with an interesting crowd lately."

"Are you envious?"

"Concerned."

"So you do care, Benbow. You really do care."

"Cut the crap, Campbell. It's not you I'm concerned about. Have you seen the headlines?"

"No, I've been working. Why?"

"Turn on your TV."

Hayden turned on CNN International. There, in full color, was the wreckage—a crumpled building, fire engines, a blonde reporter with a pained looked on her face struggling to explain the scene unfolding behind her.

"Jesus, someone blew up the building, Benbow."

"Kuipers was in there."

"You've been watching Kuipers?"

"No, I've been watching the news. Do you have any idea who it may have been, Hayden?"

"Hard to say."

"Have you heard from Cannondale?"

"No. I haven't talked to him in a couple of days. He's traveling."

"Where?"

"I think he's at his place in Bermuda."

"You think?"

"Benbow, I put words in his mouth. I don't give him

advice on what he should do in his free time."

"I'll send someone around to get you. We need to talk."

Hayden stared in disbelief at the TV screen. He needed fresh air. He grabbed his leather jacket and headed to the bodega on the corner for coffee. It was his usual place—a newsstand run by a Yemeni with a heavy New York attitude who Hayden guessed had learned his English from rap videos. He called himself "Jeff." Hayden had been in Jeff's place getting coffee and a paper when they hit Control-ALT- Delete on New York on September 11.

Hayden breathed deeply as he walked out of Jeff's place. The image of the fiery scene in Amsterdam played in his head. What the hell had happened? Just then, a windowless, silver conversion van abruptly pulled up next to the curb. A twenty-something guy leaned out the window.

Hayden immediately recognized him. It was Shelly. Hayden had worked with him several times in the past at the Agency. Despite Shelly's affinity for metal music and his Ken-doll good looks, Hayden liked him. The side door of the van slid open. Hayden could see two women in the back.

"Shall I just climb in, or do we make this look dramatic?" Hayden said.

Shelly motioned for Hayden to get in.

"I see you've added some groupies, Shelly," Hayden said, referring to the two women who were not amused.

"Hayden, meet Dierdre and Kendra. Kendra and Dierdre, meet Hayden Campbell."

"Pleasure," Hayden said, nodding to the women. "This wasn't what I had in mind when Benbow said he'd send someone around to pick me up."

"Never know if they're watching your place," Shelly said.

"I'm a speechwriter now, Shelly. Life isn't as interesting as it once was. I can't think of many people who are interested in monitoring me eating moo shoo pork and watching 'Survivor.'"

"You never know," Dierdre said officiously.

The van pulled through Brooklyn. Hayden watched the street signs. "Hey, isn't 'Uncle Liao's' near here? Good Chinese. Let's stop, Shelly, come on."

Shelly gave Hayden an eat shit look in the rearview mirror. "You two hungry?" Hayden asked the two women. No answer.

They came to a narrow street. Shelly took a hard right in front of a row of mews. A garage door lifted. Shelly pulled the van in as the door closed behind them. The van door slid open. There, standing in front of Hayden, was Benbow, as beat up and as angry as the last time they'd seen each other. The carapace of hostility the man had built around himself was as solid as ever.

"Benbow, you look marv'lous," Hayden said, doing his best Billy Crystal. "What are you doing in New York? Have you lost weight?" Shelly laughed under his breath. Benbow glared at Hayden, lit a cigarette, then turned around to walk up some stairs in a gesture intended for Hayden to follow him.

Benbow was based in Washington. The borrowed New York office was the kind of hackneyed hideaway Hayden had quickly tired of when he worked for the Agency—dark, uninteresting, stale. This one had a lumpy couch, an eddy of Styrofoam coffee cups in the corner and a photograph of the boxer Kid Gavilan having his face nearly taken off in the ring.

"You ever get tired of this life, Benbow?" Hayden asked. "I mean, the work isn't that interesting at the end of the day—stage a coup here and there, frustrate a tyrant. They all grow back, you know."

"Take a seat, Hayden," Benbow said, turning his back. Hayden sat. Benbow took one of the wooden chairs from the small center table, turned it around and sat across from Hayden.

"Pretty simple, Campbell. You stay close to Cannondale, and we'll stay close to him."

"Do I have a choice here?"

"No. As much as it pains me, you're the logical go-to on this."

"Why is it every time I try to get away from you, Benbow, you pull me back…"

"That's enough of the dramatics, Campbell."

"What's the matter, you guys running out of money—trying to get your intelligence on the cheap?"

"Something like that. You wouldn't have this problem if you hung around with the faceless crowd a bit more. You choose to mingle with this kind and you stay on my dance card. Just the way it is."

"Okay, okay. Spill it. What are we talking about here, exactly, Benbow?"

"Hard to say."

"Guess."

"Cannondale covers his tracks well."

"I suppose you can tell me now, Benbow—who did you have bugged at that meeting in Brussels?"

"None of your business, Campbell. Now there's one more piece to this puzzle."

"Ok, what's that?"

"Jagmetti."

"Who?"

"Otto Jagmetti. He's a banker in Switzerland. Fashions himself as a real fixer. Wears a bowler hat."

"What about him?"

"He's the guy who hooked Cheyenne up with Riga-Tech. We're keeping a close eye on him. I'd like you to do the same."

"I've never met the guy."

"You will in time."

"Alright, Benbow, let's have it. Who have you got working the inside at Cheyenne—Peter?"

Benbow smiled. "You."

Chapter 29

Kuipers' death rocked Brussels. Days seemed like weeks to Eatwell. He walked around in a stupor. The apartment was quiet. He had sent his manservant, Bernard, home indefinitely. He wanted to be alone. Derek had sent his condolences in a telegram from Zambia where he was doing another shoot.

The whole thing was troubling, not only because Eatwell had lost a good friend, but because he couldn't help feeling that somehow he, too, would be a target. What had happened to Kuipers had a purpose. It was no accident, but the police still had no real leads. Strangely, no group had come forward to claim responsibility as they normally did with these things. All that was left was an eerie silence, a pall of suspicion and a handful of conspiracy theories whispered over cups of coffee in the cafés.

And the memories. He and Kuipers had been through a lot together. Eatwell tried to go about his usual course of business. His friendship with Kuipers wasn't widely known, so he was spared the endless procession of well-wishers and sympathy. At work, his mind was miles away while he presided over meetings. He couldn't sleep at night, and he couldn't stop thinking that whoever killed Kuipers may now be focusing on him. *Maybe I'm just being arrogant,* he thought to himself over a solitary cup of tea at his dining room table one evening. *Maybe there's no connection between Menno's death and me at all? Maybe it*

was a botched assassination meant for someone else?
Maybe Menno was into something that I wasn't aware of?
Unlikely.

All that made sense was that Kuipers, a somewhat
obscure but powerful bureaucrat in the Dutch Ministry of
Waterworks, happened to share the same prejudices about a
piece of important technology and an American tycoon that
he did. Despite the "Any Questions?" performance, Eatwell
had thought that he had successfully contained his concerns
about Cannondale and the Cheyenne project and that he
had generally carried off a public image of impartiality. He
thought Kuipers had walked the same line. But now Kuipers
was dead.

Eatwell began to mentally go down the lineup of
suspects. The DeWeld government? Kuipers had gotten
their backs up, but that would be ridiculous. DeWeld was
mean, but he wasn't a thug.

A radical environmentalist who Kuipers may have
offended? No way. These groups had certainly resorted to
playful acts of sabotage in the past, but they generally
weren't killers. Aaron Cannondale or somebody associated
with him? Eatwell had never actually met the man, but he
felt he knew his kind—ruthless and self-righteous with a
predisposition for carrying the torch of capitalism forward.
Cannondale liked to make money, pure and simple,
regardless of the political system du jour. Would he kill? It
was hard to say.

Wait a minute, Eatwell thought. Kuipers had

mentioned that Cannondale's lobbyist, "Pettichew" or "Levichew," someone with that kind of name, had paid him a visit. The meeting hadn't sounded threatening, at least from the way that Kuipers had described it. In fact, Kuipers made it seem like he had skillfully danced around the man. Surely, being outwitted couldn't have bruised the American's ego enough to want to kill Kuipers?

He sipped his tea. Who? Who had the motive? Just then he remembered his lunch with Kuipers. The letter. Kuipers had mentioned a letter that he had received from a Russian company that was supplying Cannondale and Cheyenne with satellites. Name was "Riga-Tech." Kuipers said the letter was "odd but polite." He never expounded on what he meant by "odd." Eatwell's mind began to race. It seemed fantastic—Russian satellite company, Wild West economy, people showing up dead. Clichéd it may be, but it made sense.

The full impact of what had happened began to rain on Eatwell. Had the Russians become fearful that Kuipers wasn't going to grant satellite rights? Good God, had Kuipers said something to them? Had they heard "Any Questions?" and gotten the impression, as DeWeld had, that he, Eatwell, was prejudiced against Cheyenne? Had his slip led to Menno's death?

What about the Swiss banker that Kuipers had mentioned—Jagmetti? Eatwell had promised his friend that he would call the man, but what was the point? Kuipers said the man would be expecting his call. Eatwell rifled through bits of paper on the counter to find the number. He couldn't think straight.

Avenue de Tervuren was quiet. Too quiet. Then he heard it again, the car. Same drill. It pulled up in front of the apartment. The engine went silent. No doors, no voices. Eatwell peeked around the corner of the drapes. The same two orbs sat motionless.

He looked through his documents for the banker's number. There it was, inside the coffee table book on a piece of scrap paper between pages 89 and 90. He had used it as a page marker. Just then, he heard a noise at the front door. He ran to the kitchen to get a knife and tiptoed toward the foyer. The door knob jiggled and then began to turn. Eatwell's body coursed with adrenaline. He raised the knife into position. He was pretty good with a knife. He remembered his mandatory military duty. They had given him the full training. It had been a while, though, since he had simulated cutting a man's throat on a stuffed dummy. And he'd never actually done it on a real human being.

Eatwell moved behind the door as it crept open. A man's body passed over the threshold. Before the man closed the door, Eatwell rushed him in a clumsy attempt to put him in a headlock in preparation for the fatal slash across the neck. The man moaned and fell to the floor. Eatwell struggled to get clean access to the throat. He couldn't see the face. The man kicked and tried to bite Eatwell's hand. Something was wrong. This body, this heap, it felt familiar. It smelled familiar. It shouted, "Graham, what that hell are you doing?"

It was Derek. He had returned early from a shoot in Zambia. He looked into Eatwell's terrified eyes.

"Graham, stop. It's me. It's me!"

Eatwell pushed himself away, horrified at what he had almost done. Derek gently took the knife and set it on a table. Eatwell stood up and stared at Derek.

"I'm sorry," Eatwell said, shaking. He began to sob.

Chapter 30

Eatwell strolled into his office in the Commission with an assuredness that masked his concern about Kuipers' murder, and what it might mean for him. "Never let them see your emotions," had always been his motto. And he never did.

He was scheduled to meet with his Chef de Cabinet—an officious, difficult Frenchman named Albert Janeau, who had earned his stripes as a lawyer in the French Ministry of Foreign Affairs. Janeau was a political animal. Eatwell was impressed with his fox-like ability to maneuver in and out of tight situations. He and Eatwell had never been particularly close, but Janeau was the kind of troublemaker you wanted on your side. He also had an uncanny knack for getting into Eatwell's brain, an essential job requirement for a Chef de Cabinet, but an equally uncomfortable trait at times.

Janeau would want to discuss the Cheyenne acquisition. The Frenchman had been almost giddy in recent days about his ability to creatively find a way to keep the acquisition at bay—something that Eatwell had clearly signaled him to do. The two had never articulated their mutual disdain for men like Cannondale; it was just evident. They were both hard-core socialists. Still, Eatwell was about to severely disappoint Janeau. Things had changed. Other forces were at work. He needed to stall Janeau until he figured out how he was going to play his next card. For the first time in a long time, Graham was scared.

"Monique," Eatwell shouted out from his office.

"Yes," his secretary said, walking in.

"Could you please have Albert come in?"

"He's already here, sir," she said with a slight roll of the eyes. She and Eatwell harbored a mutual annoyance at Janeau's eagerness.

Janeau hurriedly walked into the office. "Sir," he said, almost out of breath.

Eatwell half expected him to click his heels. "Sit down, Albert."

"Thank you, sir."

"Albert, I'd like to talk to you about Cheyenne. It's important. I've seen the helpful analysis that our lawyers put together on the proposed acquisition."

"It is superb, Commissioner. There are some final details that need to be addressed, but I think we have an excellent case. It will be extremely difficult for the Americans to make a convincing argument in favor of the acquisition. Shall I take you through the details?"

"Not necessary."

"Sir?"

"It's not necessary, Albert," Eatwell said, fixing his steel blue eyes on Albert in a dissatisfied stare. "I'm not convinced."

"Sir?"

"It's leaky, Albert."

"Leaky?"

"I'm not convinced that it is going to hold up."

Albert glared at Eatwell, baffled. The legal analysis was one of the best he had ever supervised; he knew it instinctively. Something else was at play. His mind raced through the possibilities. Had Cannondale gotten to Eatwell? Was Eatwell susceptible to bribery? Was Eatwell getting pressure from somewhere else? What had changed?

"What are you suggesting, sir?"

"I'm suggesting that the lawyers take another crack, Albert."

"Can you offer some guidance on what changes need to be made, sir?"

"You're a lawyer, Albert," Eatwell shot back, "figure it out." "But sir...?"

"Albert. It's just not going to fly. Okay? See this bit here," Eatwell said, holding up his own copy of the analysis. "The whole section on the effect on the common market is flawed, Albert. Flawed. The Americans will crucify us."

"Sir, with all due respect, you've seen that section before and cleared it."

Once again, Eatwell used his penetrating eyes. He gave Albert a look that said, "Don't make me repeat myself." Albert was on the brink of implosion. Absolutely nothing was wrong with the section. In fact, Eatwell had complimented him on the good work weeks ago. What the hell was going on?

"Very well, sir. I'm not clear why you suddenly have an issue with that section, but I will have the lawyers fix it."

"There's nothing 'sudden' about it, Albert. I've taken another look at it, and I'm not happy with it. Is that difficult for you to understand? Shall I explain it further?"

"No, sir."

"Good. Now, if you'll excuse me."

"Of course."

Albert rose slowly, seething. He began to walk out of the room. "Oh, one more thing, sir," he said, pausing. He wasn't going to let Eatwell off that easily.

"Yes, Albert."

"What shall I tell the staff?"

"What do you mean?"

"What shall I tell them?"

Eatwell knew what Albert was doing. He had done it before. The Frenchman had a way of delicately letting him know that he didn't intend to shrink away, that he fully intended to add a couple of coins to the gossip machine about Eatwell's about-face around the Commission.

"Whatever you like, Albert. Whatever you like."

Eatwell swiveled his chair around to look at Rond-Point Schumann out of his window. It was a particularly sunny day in the capital of Europe. He pulled Jagmetti's telephone number from his pocket and began to dial from his cell phone.

Chapter 31

Otto Jagmetti, please," Eatwell said somewhat sheepishly.

"Speaking."

"This is Graham Eatwell. I'm calling because …"

"I know why you're calling."

"Do you, now? Well that's jolly good, then, isn't it?"

"Please accept my condolences. Kuipers didn't deserve what happened to him."

"Thank you. No, he didn't. I imagine you saw it on the news?"

"I did. Tragic."

"Now look, I'm not clear on why Menno asked me to ring you, but …"

"Because I can help, that's why."

"Help with what exactly?"

"With that annoying company, Cheyenne."

"If you don't mind me asking, Mr. Jagmetti, what interest is it of yours?"

"It's of considerable interest to me."

"How?"

"This is something that is better discussed in person. I will be in Brussels next week. Could we arrange dinner?"

"I suppose."

"Good. It's settled, then. We can finalize when I get to town."

"I look forward to it."

Jagmetti imagined the puzzled, slightly worried look on Eatwell's face as they hung up. This was going to be beautiful.

Chapter 32

Graham and Jagmetti had agreed to meet at Atelier de la Grand Ile in Brussels, a Russian place that smelled of burnt wood where vodka flowed freely and beautiful women, drawn by the smell of money, stood like statues on the arms of short, round men who resembled stuffed cabbages. A large, annoying man who meant well played a violin near people's tables.

Jagmetti arrived first, as he liked to do when meeting someone for the first time. It gave him the opportunity to absorb the place. If there was one thing that made him nervous, it was the unknown. He never quite understood why people put themselves at a disadvantage by showing up to a meeting late. He carefully placed his bowler hat on the seat cushion next to him. He never liked it to be too far away.

These Russians made him uneasy—so loud, so crass. Why couldn't they just eat like normal people? Why all the carrying on? Across the room a man with sausage fingers raised a large prawn high above his mouth to the clear amusement of his friends at the table. Jagmetti nursed a Russian Standard vodka—so clean, so pure.

"Jagmetti?" Eatwell asked quietly, walking up to the table.

"Sir Eatwell."

"Please, call me Graham. May I sit?"

"Of course."

Eatwell motioned for a vodka from one of the waiters.

"It is a pleasure to meet you, Graham. I have followed your deliberations in the mergers world since you came to Brussels."

"Have you, now? Look, Mr. Jagmetti …"

"Otto, please."

"Otto, look. I'm not exactly in the best frame of mind these days. I've just lost a dear friend. I've got my cabinet breathing down my neck about … well … breathing down my neck, that's all."

"About the Cheyenne acquisition?"

"Yes."

"Let it go through."

"What?" Eatwell said, startled by Jagmetti's directness.

"Let Lyrical acquire Cheyenne. It is the best course of action."

"Forgive me, Jagmetti, but you won't mind me saying that I think it's a bit early for you to be offering me advice on … well … anything, frankly."

"I understand. We have just met, but I get the impression that you decided to meet me here tonight for a reason. You didn't come here for petty conversation. You came here because you have a problem that you need to solve, one in which your dear friend Kuipers thought I might be helpful. So rather than chit chat, or waste your time, or even give you a shoulder to cry on, I am here to offer advice, and my advice to you, sir, is to let the acquisition go through."

Eatwell paused to take in Jagmetti's monologue. Part of him wanted to get up from the table right then and there, but the gentleman was right, he did have a problem that needed to be solved. He hated the situation he was now in, but he knew enough to know that Kuipers had given him Jagmetti's name for a reason. Besides, Eatwell had already decided to let the acquisition go through. This Swiss banker was simply confirming his gut on this.

"How did you know my friend Menno, Mr. Jagmetti?"

"I helped him with a problem once. He was a good man."

The violin player made his way over to their table. Jagmetti waved him off. "Would you like to hear my thinking on this, Graham?"

"Yes. Please continue."

"As much as it pains you, as much as every fiber of your body is telling you to block this acquisition; you must address some real issues that have been swimming in your head. Candidly, they are:

"One: Kuipers is not coming back. He would not think less of you for reversing your decision, particularly considering the circumstances.

"Two: Whoever went after Kuipers clearly wants this acquisition to happen. If anything, his death appears to have been a direct message to you. I get the impression that he would have wanted you to heed that message. You are right to think that you are probably the next target.

"Three: As you know, N-tel is looking to develop a high-bandwidth product of its own. They are one of my clients. They are desperate to understand Cheyenne's technology. If details of Cheyenne's technology were to somehow find their way into N-tel's hands and N-tel were to use its breadth and competitive advantage to take on Cheyenne … well … let's just say that knowing a good capitalist when I see one, Mr. Cannondale may be less inclined to nurture Cheyenne going forward with as much gusto as he has to date. You see, Graham, you win all the way around. You may need to do some dancing with your people in the Commission, but by doing what I have outlined you effectively get this monkey off your back. You help transform Cheyenne into a thorn in Aaron Cannondale's rib cage, and you put European technology back into European hands by effectively handing it over to N-tel."

Eatwell grinned. Jagmetti was smooth. He had done his homework. He knew which buttons to push.

"How, exactly, do you propose to feed information to N-tel?"

"You wouldn't need to worry about that."

"What do you mean I wouldn't have to worry?"

"Cheyenne is Cannondale's first real foray into Europe," Jagmetti said. "He may understand business. He may understand the North American market, maybe even Asia, but it has never been clear to me that he really understands Europe beyond his Austrian ski holidays and

Mediterranean sailing trips. Like most American businessmen, the further he gets away from home, the less confident he becomes."

"You may be right about that," Eatwell said. "I've seen it play out before."

Eatwell was pensive. A plate of gravlax with capers and onions appeared at their table, along with some grainy bread. Jagmetti delicately spread butter on the bread, placed a thin slice of the fish on top of it, and took a bite. It was his way of letting Eatwell mull over the wisdom that he had just imparted.

"So what's your motivation here, Jagmetti?" Eatwell asked, throwing back a bolt of vodka.

"Money, and boredom, I guess. Helping people fix problems staves off the boredom."

"Well, that's just splendid. I'm about to put my faith in a gentleman whose enthusiasm for helping me land on my feet isn't greed or vengeance; it's boredom."

"That, and a dislike for people like Cannondale. Besides, boredom isn't an awful motivator, is it?"

"Ok then, Jagmetti. Here are the ground rules. We never had this conversation."

"Done."

"Whatever you do, you do on your own time and in a manner that you deem fitting."

"Done."

"We never meet in person again."

"Fine, although that is unfortunate."

Eatwell raised his hand for another vodka. "What strange bedfellows we are, Jagmetti," he said, raising his empty glass in an awkward toast."

"Indeed."

Chapter 33

There was a certain resonance to it. Men chained together in the hull of a creaky, Roman ship, tethered not so much to the instrument of their burden as to one another—hopelessly rowing somewhere, anywhere, because the alternative, death, was not an option.

"You are all condemned men. We keep you alive to serve this ship. Row well, and live," the voice boomed from Braun's TV.

It could have been the refrain of any of the sonofabitches Braun had come across on the trading floor at any bank on Wall Street. But on this particular evening it was Arrius, the hard-nosed Roman officer who kept the slave galley running in *Ben-Hur*. *Goddam, Heston could act*, Braun thought to himself as he sipped a Diet Coke on his couch. Arrius had summed up a lot of things—row or be thrown overboard.

The testosterone of Wall Street occasionally got on Braun's nerves, but he put up with it because it paid. Hell, who was he kidding? He had bought into it. Like just about every other guy on the Street, he was biding his time until he arrived at his "number," his magic "fuck you" figure that would allow him to say sayonara to the Street once and for all at age 45, take up jazz guitar, buy a MiG, or move to Florence to become a cobbler. He had crunched the numbers. His figure in liquid assets was $80 million.

He had come far in a short amount of time. In his early

days as an analyst, it was pretty cut and dry. The bankers had their fancy lunches, ran their deals, and chaperoned Fortune 500 executives around the Street to unload vast quantities of equities in a dance that hadn't really changed over the decades. At that stage of his career, guys like him were chained to their desks, rowing along while people threw perks their way like Knicks tickets, or seats behind home plate at Yankee Stadium, or a constant supply of hot women and invitations to dinner at bankers' homes in the Hamptons.

Then something happened. He couldn't quite pinpoint when it was. It could have been in '92 when Tim Berners Lee introduced the World Wide Web. Maybe it was in '94 when Andreessen and Clark started Netscape, or when the venture capitalists on Sand Hill Road suddenly overtook the bankers as the big swinging dicks, or when the telecom barons set off on their odyssey to build phone networks to the sky for every man, woman, and child on the planet.

Who knew? Who cared? All Braun knew was that things had changed for him on a grand scale. Somewhere along the way, the bankers started coming to *him*. Somewhere along the way *he* was inviting the telecom barons to *his* boat and *his* beach house.

He had known what they wanted. He had known exactly what they wanted. They wanted him to throw a little positive coverage their way. They wanted him to keep the good times rolling. They wanted him to verify that it truly was a new world order, and they were shaping it with their bold, maverick moves into a cyber frontier that promised to create the kind of better, faster, more nimble world that human beings everywhere deserved.

The companies he had written about in the '90s were full of promise. They were so far out on the cutting edge that he occasionally thought it ridiculous to even attach quantifiable measures to them. It was game-changing stuff. No one ever tried to put a price tag on democracy, or freedom, or peace. *How could they?* He used to think to himself. *Wasn't it equally unrealistic to slap a price tag on the impending possibilities that the new technologies would offer? Wasn't it silly to assume that by crunching numbers and pulling together spreadsheets one could even hope to quantify what the future held—a future based on clean technologies, brain power, and meritocracy?*

For a brief period of time in the later part of the 20th century, Braun and his clients had made long-term bets that would liberate humanity from the soul-sapping yoke of doing things the way they had always been done, and nobody was going to tell them otherwise. Then the bottom fell out. But it didn't have to stay that way. Sure, he knew history never fully repeated itself, but an echo wasn't out of the question. He remained confident that the market was about to awake from its slumber, and when it did, he was going to be damn sure that he was there.

Braun turned his attention back again to the movie. Judah had won the chariot race, Pontius Pilate had commended him for "a great victory," Messala had waved off the doctor's amputation knives and hissed his last words. Now Esther was trying to temper Judah's sustained rage against Roman tyranny.

"It was Judah Ben-Hur I loved," Esther said. "What has become of him? You seem to be now the very thing you set out to destroy, giving evil for evil. Hatred is turning you to stone. It's as though *you* had become Messala! I've lost you, Judah."

"No you haven't," Braun said out loud, reaching for a bowl of baby carrots that he had put out for himself. "Judah is still hot for you, don't you worry."

Chapter 34

In 1626, Dutchman Peter Minuit was rumored to have bought Manhattan from its Native American inhabitants for $24 worth of beads and trinkets. Just 41 years later, under the Treaty of Breda, the Netherlands traded Manhattan to the English, in part, for a small nutmeg-producing island in the East Indies called Pulo Run. The Dutch also got Surinam out of the deal.

I could use a deal like the one the British got; Zlotnikov thought to himself as he sipped a Coke in a Moscow café. It was the sweet taste of nutmeg in the Coke that had gotten him thinking about the exchange between the Dutch and the English. He had read somewhere that Coca-Cola was the biggest consumer of nutmeg in the world. *Maybe nutmeg was the secret ingredient in Coke.* Go figure.

Zlotnikov waited for a call on his cell phone from one of the drivers for a big Russian tuna named General Volskov. Volskov was the man that Riga-Tech and Jagmetti had worked with to secure the communications satellite for Cheyenne.

Zlotnikov's cell phone went off. He had programmed his Nokia to play the Scandinavian drinking song "Helan Gar" when it rang. The song reminded him of some very drunken times in Helsinki when he was in his late 20s.

It was Volskov's people. The car would be there in a few minutes. Zlotnikov finished his Coke and thought about coffee-colored women on warm islands where nutmeg was sprinkled on everything.

* * * *

Hayden sat alone in Benbow's beat up, borrowed office in Brooklyn reading confidential files under a solitary light. He was pouring through background on Jagmetti, as well as General Volskov.

Jagmetti couldn't have been more different from his parents. He won scholarships to Switzerland's best schools, as well as to the London School of Economics. He didn't travel much. His clients seemed to come to him. He apparently excelled at cross country skiing. Otto didn't appear to have close friends in his life, nor did he have a woman.

General Volskov was a renowned tough guy. He had a background similar to the siloviki, the group of former and corrupt KGB officials that Putin had surrounded himself with at the Kremlin. That said, Volskov hadn't been fully accepted by them. He also had a weakness for swarthy young women from across the former Soviet Union. Volskov enjoyed entertaining such women in his dacha outside of Moscow.

Volskov had been entrusted with overseeing Russia's spent nuclear fuel. The Northern Fleet's main storage facility for nuclear waste on the Kola Peninsula was known to be leaking radioactivity, so spent fuel was being sent to Andreeva Bay on the western shore of the Litsa Fjord about 45 kilometers from the Norwegian border. Problem was, it was being stored in open concrete tanks, which were full.

Spent fuel types TK-11 and TK-18 were, therefore, being placed on the ground in containers near the overfilled tanks. The unsecured storage of the fuel violated any number of Russian and international regulations. The fear was that if something wasn't done before the upcoming winter, the containers could develop cracks from ice and snow, and radioactive material could leak into the Fjord.

Putin inherited the whole situation from Yeltsin, who had ignored it. Yeltsin had denied access to the area to experts from Norway and the U.S. It was not a headache Putin needed, so he put the thumb screws to Volskov to clean it up with the help of the Russian civilian nuclear inspection organization, Gosatomnadzor. Volskov had been pushing back, claiming he needed more funds, but Putin had made it clear that he would need to make do with what he had. And what galled Volskov most about the whole situation was that it was taking valuable time away from his private money-making endeavors, like using his position to help secure satellites for Western companies such as Cheyenne.

Chapter 35

Volskov's office was a shrine to former Soviet might. There were medals and sashes and photos of him standing proudly alongside Gorbachev, Chernenko, and Gromyko. He had a menushka doll of Ronald Reagan that got more diminutive with each layer, and a pair of Texas Longhorns mounted on his wall—a gift from an American businessman who had decided to ingratiate himself to the Russians by sending over a small herd of cattle via a Federal Express jet.

Volskov was an imposing figure at six feet, three inches tall. Slim and polished with silvery hair, he had a booming voice.

"*Sadityes, pozhalusta,*" Volskov said, offering Zlotnikov a chair. "Moscow can be hot during the summer, no?" He wiped his brow with a handkerchief.

"Too hot, General. I've come to talk about the satellite. When do you think we can get it up? The American wants it up."

"Next week," Volskov said. "This American— Cannondale. What is his situation?"

"We usually communicate with him through his people. He tends to keep his distance."

"A good businessman, no?"

"Yes."

"Don't worry about a thing. How are things at Riga-Tech?"

"Not bad. The officers of the company applaud the government's recent decision to increase satellite launches."

"Yes, I bet they do," Volskov said, slightly annoyed by Zlotnikov's sycophantic air. "Are we done, here?"

"We are. I wish you a good weekend, sir. How do you plan to spend it?"

The way Zlotnikov said it made Volskov shoot him a glare that was perhaps too revealing. Then again, maybe it was just an honest question.

"With my family, of course, in the country."

"Ah, it's a good time of year to be in the country."

"Indeed, it is. Good luck to you. You will keep me informed, no?" Zlotnikov showed himself out. It was a Friday. Volskov would indeed keep his promise to meet his family in the country for the weekend, but not before a little dalliance with a 17-year-old Uzbek girl who had recently been introduced to the good general.

Chapter 36

Roughly 8,000 man-made objects larger than a grapefruit circle the globe at any given moment. From deep inside central Kazakhstan, one of the most remote places on the planet, number 8,001 was about to be introduced.

The Baikonur Cosmodrome in Kazakhstan was built in 1955 on a barren steppe where herds of wild horses and desert camels roam.

Steeped in secrecy, the Russians had given the facility multiple names over the years to throw off the Americans— Zarya, Leninsky, Leninsk, Zvezdograd. Yelstin was the first to call it "Baikonur." In an odd bit of post-Cold War irony, the Kazakhs now claimed rights to the facility and charged the Russians $115 million a year in rent.

Baikonur, the oldest space launch facility in the world, was beginning to show its age. Paint chipped off buildings. Above all, the staff lacked the kind of camaraderie and fire that they'd had during the Space Race. Ideological verve had given way to commerce. Sputnik 1—the first satellite— was launched from Baikonur. The rocket that carried Yuri Gagarin lifted off here. The founding components of the International Space Station left from this plot of land, and yet on this particular day, the minions who worked inside the facility saw it was merely a site where a communications satellite called "Cody" was getting primed for some rich American guy with a company in the Netherlands. General Volskov had come through with the satellite, just as he had promised.

Like all elliptical satellites, Cody would make enlarged, oval-shaped orbits around the Earth.

The sky had become a crowded place at the dawn of the 21st century. LEOs or "low earth orbit" satellites circled east to west along the axis of the equator. Because they were only 200 to 500 miles up, they delivered beautiful shots of Earth. They moved fast 17,000 miles per hour—circling the world in 90 minutes. When LEOs broke down or died natural deaths, their remains added to the space graveyard of rockets, frozen sewage and bits of metal that regularly hovers above the Earth like cosmic salad.

Within the LEO class, there were Polar Satellites that circled the earth from north to south, providing information such as highly accurate weather predictions.

Further out were GEOs, or "geosynchronous equatorial orbit" satellites, which did not circle the Earth. They floated in one place over the equator, 22,300 miles up— satellite and Earth moving together in unison like a couple dancing. At certain points in the sky, GEOs and elliptical satellites get relatively close to one another.

Since Earth takes 24 hours to circle on its axis, GEOs take a full 24 hours to circle the planet. Because they are so far out in space, GEOs have a broad view of Earth. That's why TV stations use GEOs to send signals.

Dotted through various other parts of the sky are spy satellites, mainly Russian and American, which have been circling the Earth for more than 35 years. There are also GPS satellites.

The launch team at Baikonur had just finished a breakfast of eggs, peppers, and stewed meat. Cody would go up the following day. They had been busily refurbishing it for more than three months now. All that was left were some last-minute downloads and tests. Once the bird was up, Cheyenne would finally be able to fill in the gaps in its network. The launch team would spend the day at their consoles making one last check that the satellite was correctly affixed and ready to go. It was a tedious but necessary act that would ensure that the satellite settled into its orbit, faced the right direction and remained secure.

Chapter 37

It was now noon in Baikonur. Sergei Gudak, a 26-year-old from Novosibirsk, who had escaped the monotony of his timber-hauling hometown, was mindlessly entering software scripts into his computer in the air-conditioned room. He hated this part, close to the end of a satellite launch, the stage where any monkey could tap on keys just as easily as he could.

What he really wished he was doing, though, was working on the international space station in the building just across the compound. That's where his school friend, Leo, worked. That's where all the leather jackets worked. He and Leo had come to Baikonur together, but Leo had better skills. Sergei knew he would get on the space station project eventually, but until then he would have to earn his stripes with satellite gigs. Still, as lonely as it sometimes got, it beat hanging around the bars and knocking up girls back home. He ate well; he was paid well, and he was learning a skill. Occasionally, something interesting happened.

"Ok, step thirty-two," he said, turning to his partner, Vasily, next to him. "Ready?"

"Da."

Step thirty-two was a particularly tricky set of script, unlike thirty-three and thirty-four, which were a bit like breathing. Pressing a wrong key at thirty-two was more than a temporary setback. Screw it up and you ended up having to rewrite several hundred lines of code. That wasn't something Sergei relished.

Sergei and Vasily typed deliberately, methodically, mumbling instructions to one another. They scanned the code and log files for error messages. There was a sort of rhythm to the way they inserted the scripts, like riffs on a guitar. An hour later, it was done. Sergei rubbed his eyes, which seemed to have absolutely no water in them.

"I'm going to need glasses soon," he said.

"No shit. Me, too. Want to move on to thirty-three?" Vasily asked.

"Da. Let's finish."

Sergei called out instructions from the manual as Vasily tapped the commands.

"I know what to do," Vasily said curtly.

In that split second, somewhere beyond the computer screen, two young men in Yemen—Nabil and Hassan— young men about the same age as Sergei and Vasily but a universe apart—waited for just the right moment.

"Ready?" Nabil said to Hassan.

"Yes."

"Now!"

Nabil hurriedly entered the software patch as Hassan masked it with code that wouldn't raise suspicion at the other end.

Just then, an error message appeared on Sergei's screen in Baikonur.

"What's that?" he said.

"What?" asked Vasily.

"I just got an error message."

"Probably a power surge or something."

"Maybe. I hope it didn't affect the script," Sergei said, pissed off at the prospect. He scanned the lines on the screen with his index finger. "Fine ... fine ... good," he said, scrolling down. Okay. Good ... hey."

"What now?" Vasily sighed.

"That's funny?"

"What's funny?"

"Nothing. I just hadn't seen that before."

"It's fine, Sergei. Don't worry about it. I'm getting hungry again."

"Me, too. And we just ate. What's the problem with this place?"

"I don't know. I'm always hungry."

Nabil and Hassan stared at their screens in Yemen in silence, anxiously waiting for some sign of success, but no immediate sign would come. It was impossible to know if the first patch had taken. It would be impossible to know if the second patch had taken. They wouldn't know if anything had worked until the satellite was actually in its orbit.

"Patience," the old man cautioned them. "Do as we discussed. Allah will be with you."

Patience. It was the prime lesson that Nabil and Hassan had been taught in the training camps. Learning how to kill or hijack or manipulate through fear—all were secondary to patience. It was the ultimate weapon. It was their atom bomb to be dropped on the infidels at a time of their choosing—infidels too busy accumulating material things to notice. These infidels had the attention span of fish. They were like children with beards.

Nabil and Hassan had seen it for themselves when they lived in the States—people flicking through endless television channels, unfinished books discarded on bedside tables, a general anxiety about attaining exactly what they wanted. It was sad to watch such weakness. It would be a joyous experience witnessing its destruction.

Nabil had studied his software programming at Stanford. He also spent six months on an internship at NASA's Ames Research Center. Wherever he was, he excelled. His classmates expected him to do what everyone else was doing at the time—buy some black clothing and join a dot.com with other like-minded Valley Bolsheviks in hopes of doing an IPO and moving to Maui six months later. His American friends had absolutely no suspicion that he was part of a very different revolution.

It was particularly hard for Nabil in America. He would go for as long as six months without hearing from his contacts. He often wondered if his talents would ever be called into action. He didn't want to be like the old men back home, losing themselves in the perpetual haze of nostalgia, reminiscing about the one great journey they had made in their lives. He wanted action. And in those moments of despair, he contemplated going to the side of the infidels. Despite their greed, their lust, and their arrogance, he actually liked them.

Yes, patience was difficult. The longer Nabil was away from the ways of Islam, the more assimilated he became to the ways of the West. He liked going to Hollywood movies. He liked Cool Ranch Doritos and Chinese takeout. He liked the women with their white skin and big smiles. In America, most girls were willing to spread their legs for little more than a couple of beers and a sentimental song on a jukebox. Still, Nabil's soul remained still. He knew he was a soldier in a new jihad, and he looked forward to serving.

The old man understood the frustration of boys like Nabil and Hassan. Patience was always harder for the youth, which was why the boys had been plucked back. These boys were his thoroughbreds; he was their trainer. Too much had been invested. Mr. Bush's war against Islam would end in his own defeat and humiliation. The old man would be damned if he was going to let all the hard work evaporate. They would all be damned if they failed.

It was now two o'clock in the afternoon, Yemen time. The two Russians, Sergei and Vasily, had been away from their computers for lunch.

"They're back. Prepare for the second patch," Nabil said.

"Where are we?" Sergei asked Vasily. "Just completing forty-two."

"Good. Let me know when you're ready to move to forty-three." Sergei picked at a piece of shredded beef that had tied itself around one of his molars. He had reported the error message on his screen to one of his superiors over lunch, who told him it was probably nothing.

"One moment," Vasily said. Tap, tap, tap … "okay" ... tap, tap, tap … "there."

Sergei straightened in his chair, cracked his fingers, and jumped back into the river of software script. The air was becoming stale in the room. He hated this point, the point where it all became so mindless that he sometimes forgot where he was or what he was doing. He shook his head to wake himself up and slapped his left cheek.

"What are you doing?" Vasily asked, laughing.

"Don't worry about it. Okay, step forty-three finished."

They paused for a moment, then moved on to step forty-four.

"They've started on forty-four," Hassan said. "Here we go."

Same drill. Nabil downloaded the second patch while Hassan wrote masking code. They were like surgeons sewing up a patient—get it right and the scarring would be almost undetectable; get it wrong and it was there for the world to see.

Sana'a pulsed. The old man looked solemnly over the shoulders of Nabil and Hassan as they banged away on their keyboards. It was time again to pray, but prayers would have to wait. After all, they were doing this for him.

Chapter 38

Cheyene's satellite, "Cody," had settled into its orbit like a baby snuggled in its crib. In order to fully assess the satellite's capabilities, Peter had set up small test groups of 20 households in landlocked parts of Europe like Krakow, Budapest, Vienna and Prague.

Voice, video, and data were delivered to the groups 24 hours a day.

When interviewed, the participants expressed excitement combined with confusion. They had each become local celebrities overnight. Friends and neighbors crowded their houses to have a look at the device connected to their water system, and at the seemingly endless choice of channels and music.

If there were any complaints from the families, it was about information overload. Many of the families hadn't even owned a computer let alone high-speed access to the Internet. They had gone from being technology laggards to having the fastest connection times in the world. Local mayors and city officials got their pictures taken with the families. Television crews conducted interviews. Total strangers dropped by for a peek.

Peter felt only slightly guilty about getting these people hooked. Their daily television viewing time had shot up from two hours to six. In the households that previously had computers, Internet connection times went from one hour a day to four. A permanent glow of television sets and computer screens radiated from living rooms, bedrooms, and dens. Kids were spending less time playing outside and were getting fat.

Few families could have paid for the service on their own. Cheyenne was still playing with pricing models, but at a minimum, the service would cost roughly the equivalent of a monthly telephone bill, not including computers or television sets. Getting these families to give this up would be like getting them off crack.

Chapter 39

Hayden was with Aaron in Paris for a speech. He was sitting on a leather couch in his hotel room killing time reading one of Braun's analyst reports about Cheyenne. Finance wasn't his thing, but he recognized hyperbole when he saw it.

Braun's reports on Cheyenne had become increasingly, almost embarrassingly, positive. *The least he could do was tone it down a bit*, Hayden thought. Cheyenne had a lot going for it, but he knew the characters enough to know that what he was reading on paper wasn't necessarily happening in real life. The interesting thing was that none of Braun's peers forcefully disagreed with his analysis of the company.

And for good reason. Time and again Braun had proven himself to be right. Time and again, he had led the pack in identifying the early technology stars before they were born, before the rest of the slobs on the Street stumbled upon them. And he had the journalists in line.

A reporter friend of Hayden's in New York who covered the industry and was a competitor to *The Wall Street Journal* once explained how it worked. Braun had made a calculated decision to only talk to the *Journal*—no one else. Daily, Braun's phone mail would fill with requests from reporters clamoring for crumbs of gossip, insight or clarity about what was going on with particular companies. Daily, he would delete the messages. The conventional wisdom among journalists was that if you could quote Braun, your story was made.

Braun's strategy was to be pervasive in the press without actually talking to many journalists. By getting his name in one of the nation's largest newspapers, he ensured that others would simply play chase. He also ensured a certain quality control over his messaging. Because he was in such demand, whatever he said in the *Journal* would routinely get re-quoted in other publications across the country by journalists who were being whipped by their editors to match the *Journal* story. It was Braun's own private syndicate.

Hayden admired Braun's media skill. Like Braun, he didn't take many things for granted in his life, but a bet on the willingness of the crowded journalism industry to blindly match each other's stories was usually a sure thing. What an elegant deal: if the *Journal* reporters didn't misquote Braun or make him look silly, he was all theirs. If they broke that trust, it was bye-bye and a quick phone call over to the *New York Times*.

For the most part, the reporters kept it polite when covering Cheyenne. The one exception was the freelancer from Aaron's party, Tom Feegan. The blowhards on the financial TV networks occasionally interviewed Feegan about the technology universe as if he was some sort of oracle. For some inexplicable reason, Feegan came off as a lone voice of reason, always reminding investors how drunk they had gotten in the '90s. Now, he was their

designated driver, their roving reporter broadcasting live on
the Street from the corner of Fact and Fiction.

Feegan's prose had a way of gradually making monied
folk grow horns and a tail right before readers' eyes. The
TV networks sometimes allowed themselves to be taken in
by the homely heartland type taking it to the Wall Street
sharks, and in Feegan they had found their Boy Scout.

Still, Hayden had heard Braun say on at least one
occasion that Feegan didn't faze him. Sure, Cheyenne
didn't have profits, and wouldn't have any for some time,
but it had a shit pile of potential, not to mention the backing
of the sixth richest man in the world. Braun wrote that the
stock should go from $28 to $150 within a year and a half.

That sounded optimistic to Hayden. One thing that he
had noticed that Braun had clearly downplayed in his reports
was the high level of debt that Cheyenne was carrying on its
books. Nor had he noted that the timeline for fully building
out Cheyenne's network would almost certainly be longer
than the company had indicated in a previous prospectus.

Hayden's cell rang. "Hayden?"

"Yes."

"This is Libby Dunn, Mr. Cannondale's new personal
assistant."

"Oh yes, how are you, Libby?"

"I'm well, thank you. Mr. Cannondale has a message
for you."

"Sure, go ahead."

"He says you're late."

Hayden looked at his watch. He was supposed to have met Aaron for a drink at the Ritz ten minutes ago.

"Shit, you're right."

"I'm sorry?"

"My apologies. Would you be kind enough to let Mr. Cannondale know that I am running late and will join him in 15 minutes?"

"Of course."

The French cabby took his sweet time getting through traffic, and even then the guy expected some sort of tip from his American fare. Fat chance. Hayden tossed the guy the exact amount and rolled out of the back seat amid a torrent of insult.

"Good of you to make it, Hayden," Aaron said, signing a piece of paper and handing it to Pettigrew as Hayden walked in.

"Pettigrew! How the heck are you?"

"I'd be better without this damn cane."

Hayden couldn't believe the guy was even alive after the Amsterdam bombing. Pettigrew had been through the ringer—physical therapy, operations, learning how to walk again.

"What brings you to Paris?"

"He's just doing some paperwork for me," Aaron said, stepping in, giving Pettigrew a look clearly intended for him to keep his mouth shut and not share whatever they were working on with Hayden."

"Sorry to be late, Aaron. Bourbon on ice, please."

"Traipsing around the Tuileries, were you, Hayden?"

"Point taken. I was actually just reading one of Braun's reports on Cheyenne."

"Was it any good?"

"You mean positive?"

"Yes, positive."

"It was."

"I love that guy."

Chapter 40

Aaron's speech in Paris had gone well. The audience was a group of young European entrepreneurs who wanted to know what it took to become a cold-blooded capitalist, American style, in the post-dot.com world.

It had been a powerful speech. The look on the faces of the young entrepreneurs told Hayden so. To them, whatever Aaron said was gospel. How could they possibly disagree with the guy? He was wildly successful, brash, and wealthy.

Most of all, Aaron was different from their parents, and that appealed to them. Aaron represented the future, and a clean break from the stagnant drone of socialism that they had grown up with—the drone that most of their compatriots listened to every single day, never wanting more, never wishing to stick out their necks, never eager to take risks.

After the speech, Hayden and Aaron boarded separate planes. Aaron went back to the States; Hayden headed for Holland. He had agreed to go sailing with Michelle. From the vertiginous perch that Hayden's job afforded him, he was beginning to see Cheyenne's players shrink away from the headiness that had once consumed them.

Kuipers' death was the culprit. Timmermans and Peter were shaken, as was Michelle. Without saying it, they seemed to understand that other forces were at work now, forces beyond their control, and it made them nervous.

Cheyenne was no longer just an interesting idea or a way

to make money. It had transcended into something more like a stagecoach being dragged down a dusty road by a team of runaway horses. Although they now had more than 300 employees and were getting great press, none of the principals were really sure who was in command anymore. Office doors remained closed most of the day. No one met for drinks after work. Camaraderie had evaporated.

And not lost in the equation, but somewhere deep in the background, was Aaron. Neither Peter, nor Timmermans, nor Michelle had heard from him for some time. Hayden seemed to be the only one of them who had access to the great wizard. After Pettigrew's near-death experience in front of Kuipers' building, the best that Aaron could do was send flowers to Pettigrew's hospital room with a card that simply read: "Hang in there, old boy."

Timmermans, Peter, and Michelle weren't exactly clear what they would have said to Aaron had he called more often, but the fact that he didn't made them uneasy. And although they never really involved Aaron in the day-to-day running of the business, something about Aaron being the principal benefactor made them instinctively look to him for guidance, or approval, or blessing. They weren't getting any of these things.

But they were getting rich. Peter sensed that it was too good to be true. He hadn't asked a lot of questions about Cheyenne before, but he was beginning to ask them now. Peter found it strange that a company which hadn't really produced anything yet and didn't really have any customers could be so highly prized. Wasn't that the sort of exuberance that had got folks into trouble back in the '90s? Then again, what did he know? The Teestone guys were pros when it came to these things. He was just the geek.

What ate at Peter the most, though, was Braun's patronizing attitude in meetings or on phone calls. Peter wasn't a financial guru, and he knew that, but he didn't like it when Braun was sarcastic or cut him short when he pointed out problems, or delays, or just basic concerns. And in those situations when Peter spoke his mind, Braun would give Timmermans a look like "who the hell is this guy?"

It angered Peter, big time. Peter was the brain behind the company. He was the kid who spent all his time working to get the network up and running while pricks like Braun were making appointments at tanning salons. The least Braun could do was show some respect.

It was all moving too fast for Peter. He needed a break, so for a time, he returned to the people he knew best— career graduate students who stayed up late drinking beer and smoking cigarettes in cramped apartments with take-out cartons and used furniture they'd found on the curb.

The other principals retreated for a time as well. Timmermans reconciled with his wife after fessing up to the Bavarian call girl in Frankfurt. His wife had taken it harder than he expected. Conversation was difficult, dinners were mainly eaten in silence, playfulness had been abandoned.

As for Michelle, she was going sailing with Hayden.

Chapter 41

They set out on a windy, sunny Friday, sailing by the broad beaches off the island of Texel with its sheep. They passed Vlieland, and then the island of Terschelling with its cranberries and eventually the sand flats of Ameland.

Michelle loved her boat. It was a 48-foot Swan with flared topsides, a flat run aft, and a beamy, powerful stern. She easily cut through the choppy North Sea waters. Below deck, a warm, cherry interior took some of the sting out of the wind. Michelle called her *Wavelength* in honor of all they were trying to achieve with Cheyenne.

The boat was the only retreat left where Michelle felt that she had some semblance of control, although as a sailor she instinctively knew that the sea had the upper hand. Her boat, indeed her life, could be stripped away if the sea felt like it.

In their more philosophical moments aboard together, Hayden and Michelle talked about the respective anchors weighing them down from what they really wanted to do with their lives. In Michelle's case the anchors were the concept of children, and the Calvinist notion that God's grace came through financial success. For Hayden, it was a curiosity and wanderlust that prevented him from embracing any particular form of stability. At one point, they agreed that they envied each other, but also that if they were to trade places they would only be comfortable with a temporary arrangement.

Somewhere between the Frisian Islands and Denmark, Michelle came out with it. Hayden had been half expecting it. Anytime he was with her she made him feel like an involuntary ambassador for Aaron Cannondale.

"Hayden, I'm going to ask you this once."

"Shoot."

"Did Aaron have something to do with Kuipers' death?"

Hayden paused, deeply. It wasn't the question he thought Michelle was going to ask him. He thought it would be more along the lines of, "Why haven't we heard from Aaron?"

"Jesus, I don't know, Michelle. You think Aaron had something to do with it?"

"Does he have it in him, is what I mean, Hayden."

"I don't think he does."

Michelle paused. "I think you're naive. I think he's entirely capable. Kuipers was threatening to block the merger. He was in the way. Aaron is a puppeteer, Hayden. I'm supposed to be running the finances for this company, and I don't know what the hell is going on half the time. Aaron never returns my calls. I'm not told about certain meetings. Timmermans' marriage is about to implode, and those assholes from Teestone always seem to be hanging around. Peter is uncontainable. What's the point of it any longer?"

Michelle remained at the helm of her boat, looking straight ahead, stoic. Hayden faced her, perpendicular to her profile. She was sexy and tough. He wanted her. Her blonde hair blew in the wind. Her face was sunburned, her lips slightly chapped.

"Michelle, I don't have the answers you are looking for. I'm Aaron's speechwriter, not his minder."

"I know. It's just that you spend considerably more time with him than I do." Michelle began to anchor the boat. It was lunch time.

"The more time I spend with Aaron, Michelle, the less I feel that I really know him."

"Why did you take the job—with Aaron, I mean?"

"Why did you take the job with Cheyenne?"

"Bit of adventure, I suppose."

"Bingo."

"I could do with a little less adventure at the moment, Hayden. Know what I mean?" Michelle motioned to move into the cabin to have something to eat. Hayden ducked as he made his way down.

They prepared a simple spread of Gouda, olives, herring, bread, tomatoes, and a bit of wine. Hayden could see the stress in her face. She opened more wine.

"How much time have you spent with the guys from Riga-Tech, Michelle?"

"Those Latvian/Russian idiots? None."

"I was just with them."

"I know. I don't think I like Russians very much."

Hayden smiled. "Why is that?"

"Pretty significant inferiority complex going on there,

don't you think?"

"I can't disagree with you on that."

"And why did Aaron have you stay behind in Frankfurt anyway?"

"Intel. He wanted someone to keep an eye on them. That's just the way he is."

"And you don't mind playing that role?"

"It's not something I'm going to get too worked up about, if that's what you mean."

Michelle got a mischievous look in her eye. She was now sitting quite close to him. "What *does* it take to get you worked up, Hayden Campbell?" She looked into his eyes.

"Michelle … about New York … Central Park …"

She put her index finger on his lips, shook her head, and leaned in for a long, steady kiss."

Hayden pulled back for a second. "Michelle …"

She shook her head again. "No more talking, Hayden. I can't stand to talk anymore. I just need it to be quiet."

Hayden looked at her for a moment. He stroked her forehead. She was vulnerable. He knew that, but he didn't care. She didn't care. She wanted a distraction from the headaches of Cheyenne, Aaron, satellites, and Russians, and Hayden was it.

Chapter 42

Hayden was back in the U.S. and on his way to Detroit with Aaron, who had been invited to speak to a special session of the Economic Club of Detroit. The topic was what it was going to take to get the economy back on its feet. It was the kind of venue Hayden loved writing for—a high-profile audience with a serious issue at hand, the kind that would allow his client to temporarily sidestep the quotidian rituals of quarterly earnings and stockholder returns. In a world that had gone visual, it was one of the last places left where words still mattered.

After a typically flattering introduction by the chairman of a local bank, Aaron rose slowly and deliberately in the center of the three-tiered Cobo Hall dais filled with Detroit's auto moguls, politicians, and what seemed to him to be an unusual number of black Baptist pastors.

Aaron wasn't a flag waver, but he was about to give the most patriotic speech he'd ever given. He paused at the podium like an Olympic diver balancing on the platform. Then he leapt

"For many Americans, normality still feels elusive. The dust has settled in New York, but dusty coffins still arrive from Baghdad. Regardless of our respective political stripes or what we think about the War on Terrorism, we're involved. We have no other choice than to be involved—to be engaged.

"Bottom line, normality as we once knew it is gone.

It isn't coming back. You know, after September 11, I wondered how long it would take for things to feel right again. Of course, for those who lost loved ones, things will never feel right. But for those of us who didn't, I think it only took several weeks to breathe again, a testament to how quickly human beings can bounce back.

"I say several weeks because that was how long the baseball season was postponed that year. I was invited to see the Yankees play in the World Series. I went out to Yankee Stadium. I bought a hot dog and a coke and a program. There's something soothing about the act of filling in the scorecard with a freshly sharpened pencil. It was at that moment that I knew we were going to be okay. We were. And we are."

Hayden smiled. He had actually been the one at the Yankees game, but he had given the anecdote to Aaron.

"So I wonder: if people can get on with their lives the way that they have, why hasn't the market fully rebounded from the drumming it took only a few short years ago? I don't know the answer, but like you, I want that to change."

Aaron paused for effect.

"On a beautiful day in September of 2001, America and Americans became a little more complicated. We became a little older. But complexity and age need not lead to cynicism. That wouldn't be in our character. Neither is defeat. The market is coming back. We need

to keep it up.

"What concerns me, though, is that we continue to blame each other for what happened on 9/11. That's not in our national character either. Within months of the single largest act of terrorism on American soil, the recriminations began—special Congressional hearings, the "independent" 9/11 Commission, Bush is a liar, Valerie Plame, and on and on. The fact is, 9/11 did exactly what Osama wanted it to do – it divided us.

"Blaming ourselves has become the national obsession as of late. We must retrieve the unity that we felt right after 9/11. If we don't, kiss this great American experiment goodbye.

"Action is what best defines our character. At our core we are doers. And what we need to do right now is get this economy back on its feet. We are rebuilding this country again—slowly, methodically, deliberately. Corporations are licking their wounds. People are buying things again ..."

Aaron was getting a good reaction. Heads nodded. People looked at each other as if to say, "The man is right." He went on to discuss the hardships that companies would continue to face in the near term, and how it was crucial for the success of the American economy that people put their money back into the stock market, and that they carry on as they once had.

As Aaron prepared to close, Hayden saw something he hadn't seen before in Aaron's eyes—sincerity, not the kind of sincerity that executives feign to get them through annual shareholder meetings and analyst calls, but a deep-rooted sincerity that said, "I mean it."

"… The Fed is doing a good job of guiding interest rates. Europe is beginning to take growth, innovation and structural reform seriously. In my industry, demand for IT software for everything from security to collaboration is bouncing back."

The hair on Hayden's neck rose on end. Aaron was rising to the occasion as gracefully as he ever had.

"Ladies and Gentlemen, a few short years ago our country, and all that it stands for, was attacked. People still hurt, but we must look forward, not back. The construction crews and architects are rebuilding the lower end of Manhattan as we speak. The scars on the Pentagon are beginning to fade. Democracy has a fighting chance in the Middle East, and people are investing again. They are acting. I challenge you to act. Act the best way you know how. Just act."

The crowd clapped forcefully. It was a home run, and Aaron knew it.

"Well, old boy, you did it again," Aaron said to Hayden as he departed the stage.

"It was all you, Aaron."

"Nonsense. You make me look good, Hayden."

"I'm glad it worked out."

An invisible bond—the kind that rises up between people who go through a test together and come out smiling—began to swell inside both men. They turned to each other and shook hands. And at that moment, Hayden liked Aaron a lot. Aaron was cigarettes and booze and dancing all night long. Not liking Aaron was kind of like being a teetotaler. Aaron got the adrenaline running in you. He made you feel like you were flying, but just as you were about to let out a yell, he'd disappear, leave or get led away by someone in the room who wanted a quick word with him.

They took the car for the long block to the Marriott at the Renaissance Center. As they entered the lobby, Tebelis—one of the Russian Riga-Tech goons from Frankfurt—suddenly walked right by Hayden as if he'd never seen him and put out his hand to Aaron.

"You almost make me cry with dat speech of yours," Tebelis said sarcastically.

Aaron looked stunned to see Tebelis.

"What are *you* doing here," Aaron said dismissively. "We must talk."

Aaron paused and looked Tebelis up and down.

"Sorry Hayden, can you excuse us?" Aaron said, not turning his gaze from Tebelis.

"Sure," Hayden said as Aaron and Tebelis headed for a hallway near the elevator bank.

Hayden smiled. *Nothing changes*, he thought. Just then, someone bumped him from behind.

"Sorry sir," said a kid with a goatee wearing a phone company shirt and a pair of horn-rimmed glasses. He wore headphones and a tool belt big enough to take a deep sea diver to the bottom.

It was Shelly, Hayden's former CIA colleague.

The kid smiled but didn't make eye contact, just kept shuffling through papers on a clipboard and looking around as though he was searching for an outlet or something.

"Shelly? Jesus. Aren't you being a bit obvious?"

"Dammit, Hayden, keep your voice down."

"This is pathetic. Benbow's got you checking up on me while I'm supposed to be checking up on Cannondale?"

"You could say that," Shelly said. "Wait," he said, pointing to the headphones. It was a listening device.

"What are they saying," Hayden asked, suddenly interested.

"The Russian is yelling at him. Says Cannondale hasn't paid up. Dierdre, you getting this?" Shelly whispered into his lapel. "Cannondale's telling him to calm down ... take it easy. That's this guy's nickname, you know—'Easy.'"

"He's got a nickname?"

"Oh yeah, this guy is nuts."

"Why do they call him 'Easy'?"

"Because when he doesn't get his way he goes berserk. I mean crazy. The guy can snap at any moment. Two years ago, he lost it and ripped a guy's ear off the side of his head with his bare hand."

"His bare hand?"

"I'm not shitting you, Hayden. Shhh. Wait. He's saying something."

"Who?"

"Cannondale. He's telling Easy not to worry ... everything will be taken care of. Easy is telling Cannondale he better get the money soon. Oh, Easy is leaving. He's coming this way."

Hayden and Shelly moved into a hallway on the other side of the elevator bank and watched the Russian cross the lobby, straighten his tie and creak his thick neck the way Goodfellas do. He walked out the door and left.

Fifteen minutes later, Hayden met Aaron in the lobby for the trip to the airport. The post-speech euphoria was gone. He barely acknowledged Hayden as they walked out to the limo. And for the first time ever, Hayden thought he saw fear in Aaron's eyes.

Aaron and Hayden got in the car as the bellman put their luggage in the trunk. They were silent during the half-hour trip to Detroit's Metropolitan Airport. Hayden's eyes were open to the perversity of power. He really wanted to like Aaron, but he had seen the underbelly. What is more, Hayden was completely unaware of the havoc that was about to be released in a series of digital ones and zeroes from Cody's payload.

Chapter 43

Graham Eatwell looked out his office window at the minions of briefcase soldiers below shuffling in and out of the EU's bureaucratic cathedrals.

He had made his decision about Cheyenne. He was going to bless it. He had to in order to save his own neck. Though the analysis that his staff had reworked on the case was now tighter and more logical than the first version against the merger, he still had no intention of accepting it. His Chef de Cabinet, Albert, would go apoplectic. With the exception of the Dutch EU Commissioner, who shared the Dutch Prime Minister's desire to attract high-tech companies to the Netherlands, Eatwell's peers would be puzzled. It would be a tough performance, but he had been on stage plenty of times before.

"Sir Eatwell, Albert is here to see you," Monique said, peering into the office.

"Very well. Send him in." Eatwell took a deep breath and braced himself.

"Morning, sir," Albert said, walking quickly into the room. He had a smile on this face like a schoolboy who knew he had just aced a test.

"Good morning, Albert. Coffee?" Eatwell offered, pointing out the thermos and cups in the corner of the room.

"No, thank you."

"I'll get straight to the point, Albert. I've read the revised analysis. It's still not going to work for us."

Albert was stunned. The smile on his face disappeared. "We've left too many cracks for the Americans to wiggle into." Albert remained quiet in silent rage.

"Now I want you to know, Albert, no one is blaming you. I don't think it's something that you or the staff could have fixed. It comes down to facts, Albert. They have a way of getting in the way sometimes."

Still nothing from Albert.

Eatwell paused. "Albert, I'd like you to inform the chefs de cabinet at the meeting this morning."

Still nothing. "Albert?"

"Very well, sir. Will that be all?"

"Come now, Albert. You must see the challenge here?"

"The meeting starts shortly, sir. I'll need some time to prepare. Will you excuse me?"

Eatwell could see that Albert had cut the rope. From that point forth, their relationship would degenerate into a stale "yes sir, no sir" with little warmth and zero trust. It was unfortunate, but it would have to be so. Albert was replaceable; Eatwell's well-being was not.

The chefs de cabinet had their meeting. Albert reluctantly delivered the news, which sent ripples through the Commission. Had Eatwell not been so transparent in his desire to nix the Cheyenne acquisition from the start, there would be less whispering at lunchtime over veal pizzaiola and Chianti at the Italian restaurants that surrounded the Berlaymont in Brussels. Had Eatwell not built such a reputation for decisiveness, few would have taken much notice. Had other members of the Commission not harbored some of the same general antipathy toward American wealth and bravado that Eatwell did, they would not have been nearly as animated as they were right now.

But it was what it was. Eatwell would sit in a room with the other Commissioners and patiently defend his decision. He would tell them that he was no longer comfortable with the merits of the case, and that it would be wiser to let the acquisition go through and use it as a negotiating tool with the discussions they were having with the Americans on bananas and airplanes.

A German Commissioner, whose government had just denied an acquisition on the assumption that Eatwell would deny the Cheyenne deal, expressed hyperbolic shock at Eatwell's decision. Eatwell took the man to task over his lack of legal training and unfamiliarity with the facts of the case.

An Italian Commissioner called Eatwell a lapdog. A French Commissioner called him a coward. A handful of other Commissioners remained silent, either uninterested or unwilling to use their chits on this one.

The next day the Commission issued a short press release that simply said it had approved the acquisition based on the merits of the case. Eatwell led a press conference, did some one-on-one interviews with choice journalists, and then retreated to his office to dictate a letter to the U.S. Trade Representative requesting a meeting on other trade issues.

Eatwell took solace in the fact that once again, he had made the wise decision. Once again, he was the defender of Europe. By preserving his own well-being, he had ensured that he would be around to steer the EU through future battles. How selfish it would have been for him to have taken the stubborn approach. In the end, it was a good compromise. Most important, it had gotten rid of the shadows that lurked outside of his townhouse.

Chapter 44

He thought he might need a larger envelope. The materials were thick. Otto Jagmetti sat in his office in Zurich surprised at just how much information Timmermans had provided him about Cheyenne's satellite.

The Belgian wasn't a model of discretion. N-tel would be thrilled with the information. It would help them better understand the system that Cheyenne was putting in place. And the more they understood about Cheyenne, the better equipped they would be to challenge it in the marketplace.

Jagmetti passed the flap of the large envelope over the moistened sponge in the glass container on his desk. He sealed it, wrote N-tel's address on the front, and didn't include a return address. He would mail it in the morning. His phone rang. It was the Client.

"Hello. Oh yes, very good to hear from you," Jagmetti said, walking over to his window "It's quite pleasant in Zurich today, thank you very much. And how about by you? … I see. The satellite? Well, it is operating quite nicely, from what I understand. Well, thank you very much. Certainly … not a problem. My pleasure."

Chapter 45

Aaron Cannondale was in his house in Osaka when he heard the news that Brussels had approved Lyrical's acquisition of Cheyenne.

A beautiful woman named Yuri, who was part of Aaron's permanent Osaka staff, poured him a cup of green tea as he soaked in an oval wooden tub. Aaron had a smile on his face.

Elliot Pettigrew sat in a comfortable chair at the Broadmoor in Colorado Springs watching CNBC when he saw the headline roll. He called room service, ordered a shrimp cocktail and a bottle of Veuve Clicquot, sat back and said, "Hell, yeah."

Hayden heard the news upon returning from the grocery store from a message that Michelle left on his answering machine.

General Volskov was reading about the deal on the Internet in his office when Riga-Tech's Zlotnikov called saying, "Guess what? Eatwell just approved the acquisition."

"You're a bit late," Volskov shot back. "Nothing we didn't expect. Good thing you're not a journalist, Zlotnikov."

In a small Dutch town known for its herring, a groundskeeper mowed the grass around Menno Kuipers' grave.

Chapter 46

Noon, Adirondack time, December 2006. Hayden had taken some time off to do a little hiking and was making his way up the side of the mountain on a pair of snowshoes.

The fight to root out terrorists and the Taliban in Afghanistan continued. News of bombing raids was commonplace around American dinner tables. And New York had begun to compound on Hayden's brain. Even five years after the towers fell, the destruction remained vivid. Transcendentalists like Thoreau and Emerson— thinkers whom Hayden would have normally written off as self-absorbed dropouts—had taken on an increased importance to him over the past few years. As complicated and unforgiving as nature could be, the two writers made sense at the moment. For Hayden, going into the woods seemed more like a return than a dropping out. He had a backpack, a GPS device, some water, and a couple of protein bars. He liked the sound of the snow crunching underneath his snowshoes. The air froze his nostril hairs. A weak winter sun warmed his face as he rounded a bend.

Hayden spotted a female white-tailed deer inching her way into an opening in the woods. She was big. Hayden sat down on a log. She still hadn't seen him, but she could smell him. Her wet black nose wiggled in the air, trying to zone in on him. Hayden remained as still as a mannequin until his right snowshoe slipped slightly from its resting position on a rock. The deer darted away, stopping momentarily under the cover of the woods to look back at him.

Hayden smiled and began to play with his GPS device. He was going to do some bushwhacking off the trail. It was a game that he'd played plenty of times before. The idea was to get completely lost and use the device to guide yourself out. He liked the risk of surrendering to the technology. He was fascinated by the concept of satellites far overhead guiding him out of peril, telling him the correct way to get from A to B when every instinct was to do the opposite.

The GPS device had saved Hayden before. A friend had once told him jokingly, "Feel the GPS, Hayden. Let it speak to you. Let it guide you. Don't disrespect it. It knows better than you do which way to go." And in those moments when the fog rolled in, or the rain poured down, or darkness fell, the friend had been right.

Hayden programmed the device, making the large boulder to his right home plate. Whatever he got up to, the GPS would guide him back to that boulder. He tied his bootlace, took a deep breath, and headed off the trail into the woods.

The snow was deep, sometimes rising up to his thigh. He had to slow his pace. He looked directly above into the blue sky. Even up in the mountains, even now, several years after the fact, he couldn't shake the image of that second plane dropping out of a benevolent blue sky and slamming into the World Trade Center.

That's what he hated most about the whole act. Somehow they had permanently taken away the innocence of the sky. Up until that day, blue skies were inherently good to Hayden, a protective dome. But having seen the destruction for himself, he knew that sinister elements now lurked behind that blue curtain, willing and ready to descend. Scratch it up to growing older or being overly sensitive, but it was just one more thing that ticked Hayden off.

He continued walking. As he walked, his thoughts wandered to childhood—childhood and evolution. It occurred to him that when you're a kid and every other kid around you with a few exceptions has a mother and a father and a bully older brother, and you all play ball together and eat the same tuna casserole that your mothers serve for dinner and every other guy has a queasy feeling in his stomach for a girl named Lisa, you tend to think that the world evolves all at once, in unison.

Then you grow up and realize that sometimes not having a mother or a father can be a strength, or being teased can make you more determined, or that having sex at 16 didn't stunt your best friend's growth, or that being a Boy Scout isn't always what is needed, or that everything you thought was right and normal was actually wrong and abnormal and didn't prepare you very well. And it's right about then that you realize that there's little morality attached to evolution, just a glacial move forward.

Hayden stopped to watch a hawk glide overhead. He

tightened his snowshoes and set off again. The even deeper here. He could only take between ten and twenty steps before he had to stop and catch his breath. He laughed at himself and his situation. Clouds began to move across the sky, the sun slaloming in and out. The temperature dropped. Hayden was now in the middle of the ridge in a sort of no man's land equidistant between the point he had left and the place where he was heading. He pulled his hat down a little tighter over his ears, fixed his scarf, and decided to push ahead.

According to the GPS device, if he continued to the other side and looped around, he could follow the river back to the boulder. That didn't seem right to him, but he wasn't going to challenge the GPS. Besides, if he got to the other side of the ridge and the weather was bad, there were overhanging rocks. He could protect himself and wait it out. He still had a good six hours of sunlight left in the day.

Just then, a fresh snow began to fall—big flakes. His strides became heavier, more laborious. His breathing picked up. The wind began to twirl the falling snow around him like a blender. He stopped to check the GPS. It indicated that he was still pretty much on target. He forged on, whipping his face, snot rolling out of one of his nostrils. The point was in sight. Another 20 minutes or so and he'd be there. He stopped again to catch his breath and to check his watch. He took a swig of water from his canteen and pushed on. The wind was steady now, and getting stronger. His cheeks were turning numb. Hayden looked back. He could no longer make out the point under the spruce tree where he had set off. Things were rapidly entering the white-out stage. He brushed snow off the GPS screen. A couple quick steps to the left and he would be on target. Just then, his right leg became stuck in the deep snow. He stopped to dig it out. By now, the blue sky that had enticed him to traverse the ridge had picked up and gone home.

Almost there, he thought. He found that if he closed one eye and squinted, he could make out where he was going. The snow came from every direction now, even from beneath him the way he remembered the rain doing once when he was at the top of the Empire State Building. He lost his footing and fell forward into a pillow of snow. Freeing himself was not a simple matter. The snow was like quicksand; the more he struggled the deeper he sank.

He tried to roll onto his back and dig the snowshoes into the ground, but there wasn't any ground. It was hard to believe, but he had entered a place where the snow was taller than he was. He positioned himself upright. Slowly he began to move the shoes as if he was walking up a flight of stairs, one foot, then the other, slowly. He continued until he freed himself. He caught his breath, got up, and walked a couple paces.

Hayden's heart raced. He leaned against a tree, exhausted. He couldn't see more than ten feet in front of him. He checked his coordinates to pinpoint the boulders that he had programmed into the GPS earlier. The boulders were big enough to have crevices he could slip into or even caves.

It was getting prematurely dark now. The GPS had a backlight, thank God. According to the machine, the boulders were about 50 yards southeast of where he was standing. But Hayden was certain that they must be farther than that. He reached for his canteen, opened it and took a swig of water. He needed to make it to those boulders if he was going to get through this thing. And so, he set off again, but this time slightly worried. He was doubting himself, or the machine—either way, he didn't like doubt. He held onto tree limbs and young evergreens until there were no more to hold. He paused for a second. It felt like he was in an open field with no boundaries. He closed his eyes and looked at the GPS again. It told him to walk to the right.

Hayden followed the coordinates exactly, walking until he could no longer feel the crunch of the snow beneath his feet. That was the last thing he remembered.

Chapter 47

Fresh off the tanker's teat with a full bag of gas, LT Pete Rand thought of the effort it had taken him to get to this point as a Navy navigator and radar intercept officer. This was his nugget cruise—his first combat mission. He was going into Afghanistan. Part of him wanted to write it all down as it was happening, but that wasn't going to happen. He needed to be focused, and he needed a good pilot. Luckily, his good friend LT Paul Simone was sitting in front of him in the cockpit.

Rand's job was to operate the aircraft's weapon systems in order to put the right ordnance on the right target. Tonight they were carrying a full load of JDAMs or GPS-guided weapons. They had a little time to kill while en route.

"So tell me again, *why* the hell did you get married *before* going on deployment?" Simone asked, laughing.

"I don't know," Rand said. "I guess it was important to lock in a good thing. Plus, she's hot."

Simone laughed as he keyed the mic. "Yeah, I supposed you've clued her into the fact that you'll never see each other?"

"No."

"Don't worry, you'll be able to blame the Navy for f-ing up her career."

Simone and Rand had been buddies since the Academy, and they stayed in touch throughout flight school. They wound up in the same fleet squadron after finishing their respective training tracks. Now they were crewed together for their first combat mission.

For tonight's flight, CDR Toby Collins was their lead aircraft. He was the squadron's XO, and he had a no-nonsense reputation born from years of combat flying.

As the two aircraft pressed toward their assigned kill-box, Collins called for a fuel check. "Voodoo 11, Voodoo 12, 17 point 5, good tapes, good feeds." The precisely formatted statement was also Collins' request for information from his wingman, LT Simone.

Periodic calls like this were also made in order to ensure that no one became complacent during these long missions.

"Voodoo 12, Voodoo 11, 17 point 6, good tapes, good feeds," Simone responded with his serious voice.

The flight was now far enough into Afghanistan that Collins could contact the local command network. Collins keyed his mic, hoping something interesting was going on. "Long Horn, Voodoo 11 checking-in, flight of two Tomcats proceeding to kill-box Tango Bravo, awaiting further instructions."

"Voodoo 11, Long Horn, contact Raven 89 on his freq, how copy?" There was an imperative tone in Long Horn's call.

"Voodoo 11, copy all, switching." Collins was familiar with the Raven call sign. Raven was a Predator, an unmanned aerial vehicle, so there was no telling where the operators might be. They could be local; they could be back in the States. Either way, chances were good that they had their eyeballs on something good.

"Raven 89, Voodoo 11 checking-in," Collins said.

"Voodoo 11, Raven 89's got you loud and clear. Stand by for a SitRep."

Raven 89 was definitely not local. The delay in the transmission and the strange side tones meant that his voice was being bounced from a post far from here. While Voodoo flight waited intently for the situation report, Simone looked out from his canopy to the complete darkness in front of him. He didn't know it, but somewhere down there a woman was making soup for dinner. Her husband played with their baby girl in the corner of their small house made of mud and straw. Their boys, one eight, the other ten, played outside. A donkey was hitched to a tree in front of the house. Thirty people lived in their tiny village—thirty people, one water well, several farming plots, a raisin-collecting silo, and a radio transmitter constructed by the Taliban that was off limits.

Recently, jets in the sky overhead had transcended from science fiction to commonplace for the oldest boy. His friends said the planes had come to punish the unbelievers. The jets normally flew by on their way to the larger cities. They had no business with his tiny village. Often, the planes flew so high that the boy could only hear them.

But today, the planes were getting louder. They had never been this close. Even his mother was surprised as she came outside to have a look.

"Voodoo 11, Raven 89, SitRep as follows; we're currently looking at a radio tower that we would like you to take out. This is a CENTCOM Priority One tasking that needs to be serviced immediately, how copy?"

Collins knew that if Raven was talking directly to CENTCOM, there were a lot of people watching this happen, real time.

"Raven 89, Voodoo 11, copy all, standing by for 9 Line."

Raven passed all of the target's information via the 9 Line format and Voodoo flight put that information into their targeting systems. So far, all was going smoothly. Regardless, anxiety was starting to creep into Simone and Rand's cockpit.

"Ok, those coordinates look good; that's exactly what I wrote down," Simone reassured Rand.

"Yeah, I think it's good. I want to double check in the INS, make sure we have a stable platform." Rand was trying to use every second he had available.

"I can't believe they want all four JDAMs on the same target," Simone said.

"Yeah, I guess they really want to …"

Simone and Rand's conversation was cut short by Raven 89 directing them to commence their attack and issuing release authority.

"Voodoo 11/12, Raven 89, push from your current position. You are cleared hot."

"Raven 89, Voodoo 11/12, pushing." Collins looked

out from his canopy to see Simone in position. Good. Now he could really focus on triple checking his systems as well.

"Holy shit this is happening," Rand said to Simone over the ICS. "I know, I know. We're good; everything looks good," Simone said to Rand and to himself.

At CENTCOM, almost 8,000 miles away in Florida, everyone's attention had shifted to the final moments of the strike. On the big screen, they could see the position of the two Tomcats and the Predator. They could also see the live video feed from the Raven 89. This area in Afghanistan was desolate, so there should be little to no collateral damage. That made the big commanders very happy. Nothing worse than having the strike you authorized on CNN.

In the final moments before weapons release, one of the targeteers on the CENTCOM floor was doing his thing. Though new to the intelligence officer community, LT Reyes was head and shoulders above many of the targeteers with more experience. Adept at all of the digital processes and computer software used by targeteers, he still liked to plot missions against charts. While all of the others watched the big screen, Reyes precisely plotted the latitude and longitude. Accounting for magnetic variance and seasonal isogonic lines, he realized something was wrong. The GPS-generated coordinates were in error. He didn't know how and he didn't know why, but those bombs were definitely not going to hit the target. With chart in hand, he stood up from his station and looked at the big screen. The small icons representing Voodoo flight were getting awfully close to the target. At that moment, he heard Raven 89 relay Voodoo's status to CENTCOM.

"Voodoo flight reports 30 seconds to weapons release." Raven's update was pumped out over the loudspeaker.

Reyes could see the battle watch captain from across the room. He was taking a pull of coffee as he eyeballed the screen. He was the man who had the final say for a mission to be a "go" or a "no-go." He was a necessary check and balance in the kill chain, and in times like these, a voice of reason. Reyes knew he had only a few precious seconds to convince him to call off the strike. As he started running across the room with his chart in hand, he knew his choice of words needed to be specific. Short of breath, he threw the chart down on the desk in front of the captain.

"If you don't call off the strike, you're going to kill a village," Reyes said, pointing his finger at the target's location on the map.

The battle watch captain stared at Reyes and took a moment to process the information. Without asking a question, he keyed the PA system on the floor and issued the order.

"Abort, abort, abort! I repeat abort the mission!" All eyes on the floor looked at him for a moment. The room erupted in a wave of noise. In the chaos, the battle watch captain looked down at LT Reyes and said, "Ok, let's talk."

High above Northern Afghanistan, the order to abort had not yet reached Voodoo 11/12. CDR Collins and LT

Simone had already armed their aircraft and were only a few seconds away from release when Raven 89 called.

"Voodoo 11/12, Raven 89, abort, abort, abort! How copy?" Raven's voice was hurried.

"Raven 89, Voodoo 11, copy abort," Collins responded with his trademark, business as usual demeanor.

"Raven 89, Voodoo 12, copy abort." Simone's disappointment was not as well hidden.

On the ground, the boy looked up at the sky. He could see the light of the jet engines flickering as they passed overhead, going back the way they had come. They must have realized that his family were believers.

Over the ICS, Rand and while making their way back to the ship. What the hell happened? It wasn't until the debrief and a discussion about a problem with the GPS constellation that Simone realized just how close he had come to killing 30 people.

Chapter 48

Sergeant Mike Murphy was the JTAC in a nine-man special ops team that was about to parachute out of a plane moving over the foothills of the Hindu Kush in Afghanistan. Once on the ground and assembled, his responsibility was to establish communications with the local command network and guide U.S. pilots overhead for a bombing mission. A group of 50 Taliban had been spotted creeping back into the northern Afghan city of Mazar-e-Sharif.

Murphy was the last one out of the plane. He was pumped. In his head blared the U2 song "Elevation." The words didn't make a whole lot of sense to him, but the melody made his adrenaline course. The cold air hit Murphy in the face. He could see shoots beginning to open beneath him now. In a moment, his would open, too. In the meantime, he relished the peace.

Peace gave way to a slight twinge of fear. On the ground, Murphy and the team made a lengthy trek to a burned-out field where American aircraft had already destroyed an ammo depot. They had received intel that the Taliban planned to rendezvous there, and were now visualizing a group of them.

In this region of the country, the command network's call sign was "Wild Cat"; Murphy's was "Panther 12." He reached for his radio. "Wild Cat, this is Panther 12, over." He adjusted the volume to squelch simultaneously. It was second nature to him now.

"Panther 12, this is Wild Cat. Go ahead with your check-in." Wild Cat's voice was British and female. Murphy guessed she was an Eastender.

"Wild Cat, this is Panther 12. Established point Lima. Request immediate air support for a fire mission, over."

"Panther 12, Wilco, ETA plus 10 minutes."

Wild Cat's voice was a calm reassurance to Murphy that a definitive force multiplier was on the way. Between now and then, the task at hand was to determine the specific coordinates of the target.

Looking through his Lightweight Laser Designator Rangefinder (LLDR), Murphy could see the Taliban beginning to muster for an offensive. Firing the invisible beam of laser energy, his LLDR was instantly able to correlate its own GPS position to that of the enemy and derive the target coordinates. Now it was just a matter of waiting for the aircraft to check in.

High above, a section of Tomcats was getting word that their services were needed. The lead pilot was a guy named York. His call sign was Ajax 31.

Murphy got on the net. "Ajax 31, this is Panther 12. We have troops in contact located in kill-box Romeo Sierra. Proceed immediately and contact Panther 12 for further instruction."

"Copy all. Proceeding to Romeo Sierra," York said from his cockpit. He plugged his afterburners and put Romeo Sierra on the nose. He knew the terrain in the north very well. He had flown there many times. It was rugged and unforgiving for the soldiers on the ground, but from the air, the backdrop of the Hindu Kush was sublime. They were close to the target. ETA was eight minutes.

"Panther 12, this is Ajax 31," York said. Silence. He listened intently for anything that sounded like a voice, but only heard static in his headset. He tried again, this time more abruptly. "Panther 12, Ajax 31." Just as he was about to make another transmission, he heard the familiar crackle of someone keying a mic.

"Ajax 31, this is Panther 12." It was Murphy. He was okay. "Proceed with your check-in."

"Panther 12. We've got you broken but readable. Ajax 31 is a section of Tomcats currently five minutes out, each carrying two by GBU-12, two by GBU-38, and 1,000 rounds of 20 mike-mike. Playtime one hour. How do you copy?"

Murphy sensed the Taliban guys were about to make their move. "Ajax 31, Panther 12. Copy all. Stand by for hasty 9-line." "Hasty 9-line" meant Murphy wanted a bomb on the ground ten minutes ago.

York got on his mic. "Panther 12, this is Ajax 31. Ready to copy."

Murphy started spewing out coordinates. "Ajax 31, this is Panther 12. Target location 36 degrees, 42 minutes, 31 decimal 7349 seconds North; 67 degrees, 6 minutes, 54 decimal 4265 seconds East, elevation 1,451. Troops in the open. Closest friendlies 2,000 meters South. How copy?"

York inputted the coordinates into the weapons system on his aircraft's data entry pad. Everything looked good. Checked. Double-checked. "Panther 12, this is Ajax 31. Ready for read back?"

"Ajax 31, go ahead."

"Panther 12, Ajax 31. Target location 36 degrees, 42 minutes, 31 decimal 7349 seconds North; 67 degrees, 6 minutes, 54 decimal 4265 seconds East, elevation 1,451. Troops in the open. Closest friendlies 2,000 meters South."

"Ajax 31, this is Panther 12, good read back. The enemy is hunkered down in an open position at the bend of a river, oriented north to west. That river then extends into rising terrain. Friendlies are south of that position. You are cleared from present position to commence your attack. Make your attack axis east to west."

"Ajax 31, copy all. East to west attack axis. Ajax 31 is pushing," York said. His "pushing" call meant the game was on. After triple checking the coordinates, there was nothing left to do but wait for the final clearance from Murphy and then push the little red button for weapons release.

"Panther 12, this is Ajax 31. Two minutes out."

"Ajax 31 – cleared hot!"

"Cleared hot" meant bombs away. Murphy had called in the strike. Now less than five miles to the target, York could just make out the bend in the river that defined the enemy's position. Check. One minute to release but something seemed out of place. Attack axis was correct, coming in from east to west. Check. York scaled in on his situational awareness display to take a closer look at the target's symbology. Now thirty seconds to release. The moving map and the target didn't correlate. York thought to himself out loud; there must be some display error here, that target looks …

Suddenly his headset erupted with what sounded like gunfire. On the ground, Murphy and his team were now under attack from the enemy's position. Yelling into his mic, Murphy called York.

"Ajax 31, Panther 12, say your status!"

"Ajax 31, 15 seconds to release." A swell of doubt started to build inside York. Something was not quite right. He needed more information. He needed more time.

"Ajax 31, this is Panther 12. Put that ordnance down range now!" Murphy yelled.

"This is Ajax 31, copy all!" *Shit, shit, shit.* After making a mental coin toss, York reasoned that it must be an error in the display.

"This is Ajax 31, one away." The knot in York's gut just got bigger. The weapon he had released had a time of flight of approximately sixty seconds.

On the ground, Murphy yelled to his team that a bomb was on the way. Welcome news that would hopefully silence the enemies' machine guns. "Everyone keep your head down; less than a minute until impact!"

From his crouched position, Murphy tried to hear the faint whistle of the bomb guiding to impact. At first, he could hear nothing except the clack-clack of intermittent gunfire. Then, he could just start to make it out. It was getting loud, too loud. The whistle became a deafening howl as the percussive thud of detonation rattled him.

"My God," he said, just as a blinding light, a shock wave, and then a flood of heat snuffed out his life.

* * * *

Hayden dangled in a basket, attached to a cable as he was being raised into a helicopter. He had walked right off the side of the ridge and fallen into a ravine. Luckily, another hiker below witnessed the fall and built a makeshift shelter for the two of them to ride out the storm until they could place a cell phone call to the mountain patrol. Hayden had a badly sprained ankle, two cracked ribs, and a bruised ego. He was confused. *What the hell had, happened? How could the GPS have been so wrong?*

High above, something had indeed happened. A GPS satellite was spitting out wrong information.

Chapter 49

It was winter in Zurich. Otto Jagmetti loved this time of year—a time for reading and drinking warm drinks, a time for getting the skis out and lighting the fire.

These years following September 11 had been a time of schadenfreudic satisfaction for Jagmetti. Finally, the Americans had gotten what was coming to them. All the years of duplicity and empire building in the name of freedom and liberty, all the self-interest cloaked in a Yankee noblesse oblige to defend the world from any of the nefarious ills that it had brought upon itself, all had come tumbling down.

Yes, a large number of people had died, and that was tragic. But for the first time in his entire life, Jagmetti felt that he was witnessing American vulnerability. It was his sincere hope that the attacks and the drumming the Americans were taking in Iraq would spell change—change in the way that America viewed the world and its place in it. To Jagmetti, it was as if an overconfident teenager used to getting his way had received his first humbling playground beating.

Admittedly, Jagmetti was as startled as anyone by the magnitude of the destruction he had seen on the television screens, by the bodies raining down onto the concrete. But what was the whole event in the grand timeline of human history? Why did that event deserve more tears than the six million Jews killed in the Holocaust, or the seven million

Ukrainians starved by Stalin, or the one and a half million Armenians massacred by the Turks in 1915-16, or the young men and boys forced to watch their wives and mothers raped during the war in Yugoslavia, or the hundreds of thousands hacked to death with machetes in Rwanda?

To Jagmetti, what happened to America amounted to a loud knock on the door from the rest of the world, a knock that said, "Get over yourself." But as a businessman, the war on terror meant something else to Jagmetti. In hockey, it was a "power play"—America was being penalized and was playing shorthanded.

Now was the time for Europe to capitalize. The window of opportunity would be short, but Jagmetti had every intention of rushing through it. To him, the historians would one day write about September 11, not as the defining moment when a new foe called terrorism replaced Communism and Fascism, but as the moment when America's hegemonic halo began to fade, once again giving others a chance to play.

And so, Jagmetti took particular pleasure doing what he had promised Eatwell he would do—send a steady stream of information about Cheyenne's technology to its closest competitor, N-tel.

It was all coming together nicely. Beyond helping Cheyenne secure the Russian satellite from Riga-Tech, Jagmetti had forged a solid relationship with Timmermans. Sometimes, feigning a deep interest in the technology, Jagmetti would ask Timmermans for a few more details.

Timmermans was always forthcoming.

Jagmetti had also gotten Eatwell to reverse his decision on Lyrical's acquisition of Cheyenne. And the Client, whom he only knew by the Swiss IBAN number CH10 00230 00A109822346, was very pleased that Jagmetti was able to give him a heads up when Cheyenne's satellite was launched, pleased enough that he had sent Jagmetti an antique fob watch on top of his fee. Yes, things were coming together nicely.

It was late in the day. Jagmetti neatly stacked the papers on his desk and walked over to the open safe. He had a clean desk policy. Every night, without fail, he took whatever was on his desk and put it in the safe. He placed the papers inside, slammed the heavy door shut, and turned the combination dial several times.

His stomach growled. He craved veal. Zürcher Geschnetzeltes—that's what he would have for dinner. He loved how his mother used to make it with mushrooms, onions, and just a bit of paprika. Yes, that's what he would have for dinner.

Chapter 50

The Langley crowd had been alerted to the GPS problems. All the intelligence agencies were having a difficult time figuring out the cause.

CIA programmers had broken off into two teams—one dealt with the bad information emanating from the satellites, the other with what appeared to be a security breach at the National Geospatial Intelligence Agency (NGA). The mapping agency had an enormous database of satellite-generated targets upon which the Department of Defense, the Pentagon, and the CIA depended heavily.

In the thick of the headiness was Benbow. Two programmers called him over.

"What?" Benbow asked.

"Sir, it's a significant breach. They appear to have access to images in Afghanistan," the programmer said, continuing to type. "They also …"

"Jesus. Ok, do what you need to do. Maureen, get CENTCOM for me," Benbow barked, pacing.

"Sir, CENTCOM is on the line."

Benbow picked up a nearby phone and peered at a computer screen over the programmer's shoulder.

"General. In addition to the GPS problem, there's a security breach at NGA."

"How bad?"

"Bad, General. They've had access to our Afghan maps. Also Saudi."

"Saudi?"

"Yes sir. Any of our planned strikes in Afghanistan could be in jeopardy."

"What's the recommendation, Benbow?"

"Suspend all sorties until we can verify to what extent we've been compromised."

"How long will that take you?"

"Forty-eight hours."

"Make it less. Keep me posted."

Benbow hung up and rubbed his eyes. For a whole host of reasons, some vague, others clear, he really did not want to make the next call that he was going to make, but he knew he had to.

Chapter 51

Hayden arrived at Benbow's office at the designated time. "Here's the situation, Hayden," Benbow said, taking his usual interrogation position by leaning on his desk with one buttock. Shelly sat on a couch.

"You didn't see any of this in the headlines, but we're losing good men for bad reasons in Afghanistan. We've got sorties being aborted and special forces teams calling in airstrikes on themselves. Three days ago, we lost an F14 and a refueler. From what we can tell, there's a thread."

"What kind of thread?"

"GPS," Shelly said. "There's a problem with GPS data coming from the satellites, Hayden."

"What kind of problem?"

"Bad information, just plain wrong," Benbow said, standing up to pace.

Hayden had a flashback to being slowly lifted in the basket after his snowshoe hike. He winced and held his side. Ribs still hurt.

"Benbow, do you think …?"

"Your accident in the mountains? Could be related, yes."

"What's causing the problem?"

"We think it's another satellite," Benbow said calmly.

"Are you serious?"

Benbow looked to Shelly to provide the explanation.

"From what we can tell, Hayden, there's interference

coming from another satellite—we think a communications satellite. We've never seen this type of GPS spoofing before. Whoever is doing this isn't just jamming GPS signals."

"What are they doing?" Hayden asked.

"They've somehow figured out a way to feed the GPS satellite fake GPS signals …"

"And then the GPS receiver thinks the fake signal is actually the true GPS signal from space …" Hayden said, finishing Shelly's sentence. "Amazing. And the receiver then calculates the wrong position or time information based on the false signal."

"Exactly," Shelly said. "We've got a rogue satellite on our hands."

"Unbelievable," Hayden blurted. "Have they been able to pinpoint it?"

"That's why you're here," Benbow said, stepping in. "We think the rogue may be the satellite that Cheyenne launched."

Hayden let the words sink in. "But how? I mean … do you think … Aaron or Timmermans ..."

"The only thing we suspect Cannondale of being is an opportunistic son-of-a-bitch," said Benbow. "He had no motive to knowingly get involved with this kind of science fiction." Again, Benbow looked to Shelly to provide the details.

"From what we can tell, someone got their hands on the satellite before it went up," Shelly said. "Security at

Baikonur is like a sieve these days. But we don't think anyone actually made physical contact with the satellite."

"What do you mean?" Hayden asked, confused.

Benbow stepped back in. "What he's saying, Hayden, is that we think someone hacked into the satellite."

"Remotely?"

"Yes, through a software patch."

"But what about our encryption?"

"Within our facilities, yes, but we're dealing with a rental property in the middle of a steppe in Kazakhstan run by a government with no budget," Benbow said. "Those boys over at Baikonur have let things slip a bit. It's not anthems and motherland bullshit anymore. They're fighting for scraps. The launch pads in Indonesia and French Guiana are stealing their customers."

"Who did the hacking?" Hayden asked, turning to Shelly.

"We're not certain."

"Do you have any leads?"

"Nothing conclusive. We've been scouring the voice intercepts from Afghanistan, Pakistan and Saudi Arabia."

"And Syria?"

"And Syria, yes."

Hayden became pensive. "You know geography is irrelevant with these kinds of things."

"We're aware of that, Hayden, but we had to start somewhere," Benbow said, pouring himself a cup of coffee.

"Why haven't you just gotten the Baikonur guys to

disable it?"

"Because if we take out this bird, the hackers will just move onto another one, and we risk losing the trace. We want to get these bastards by the tail before they do any more damage. The trick is not to let these assholes know we've found them out. I want us in and out of there. Not even the Russians will know. We can't afford to screw this up."

"In and out of where?" Hayden asked, puzzled.

Benbow paused and looked at Shelly. "We picked up an intercept in Yemen. We've got our boys studying it a bit more, but so far it's the best lead that we have."

"What kind of intercept?"

"Bill Tully, our man in Sana'a, picked it up. You remember Bill?"

"Of course. Love that guy."

"It's still fuzzy, but whoever is doing the hacking seems to know what they are doing. We need to send some folks in, Hayden."

"Who?"

"A Delta team."

"Delta, huh? Seems to me we've been down that route before. They're not bulletproof, you know, Benbow."

Benbow knew what Hayden was talking about. He didn't want to be reminded. When Hayden was still with the Agency, Benbow had sent him, another agent and a Delta team for a one-off in an African country to hack into the files of the foreign minister. They wanted to blackmail him.

Through a series of miscommunications and bad intelligence, one of the Delta boys was gunned down. Hayden barely got out with his head still connected. He remembered the peaceful look on the dead soldier's face as the body swayed back and forth over another soldier's shoulder in front of him -- that face with the dead stare looking right at him as they made their way to the riverboat.

Hayden shook his head. "I'm not going to Yemen, Benbow."

"No, you're not Hayden. You're going to Europe."

Chapter 52

Hayden packed his bags. His near-death experience in the Adirondacks, the ongoing odyssey of Cheyenne, Michelle—it was all washing over him. That, and the fact that he had drunk his client's Kool-Aid. When he went the speechwriting racket, he swore to himself that he wouldn't let that happen, but it had. He was ticked at himself. Hayden had never had any misconceptions about his role as a hired pen, because at the end of the day, that's what his clients paid him to do, but Aaron had won him over. Aaron had put his arm around him and said, "Follow me," and Hayden had.

After Aaron's speech in Detroit, Hayden could no longer discern what was real or wasn't real about Aaron anymore. Rumors were beginning to circulate that some creative accounting was going on at Cheyenne. Hayden didn't know if Aaron was guilty, innocent, or just a bystander in Cheyenne's great leap forward. It didn't really matter anymore. Hayden's cell phone rang.

"Hayden, it's Feegan. Tom Feegan. Surely you remember me—from Aaron's Cannondale's lame party out in Salt Lake."

"Yeah, Tom. What can I do for you?"

"I'm sorry to trouble you, Hayden, but I wanted to talk to you about Cheyenne."

"What about it?"

"I'm hearing things."

"Oh?"

"Yeah, bad things."

"Is that right."

"Yeah. Now, you seemed like a pretty reasonable guy when I met you, Hayden. I know that whatever may be going on at Cheyenne, you're not a part of it, but I'd like to meet up for a beer and a chat if I could."

"What do you want to talk about exactly, Tom?"

"Just what you've seen since you've been there. Just a little color, that's all. I'm sure that you're going to want to distance yourself from this thing, and I just thought … well …"

"You thought, 'What the hell? I'll give the speechwriter a call and see if he'll just roll over on his back like a Collie,' is that it, Feegan?"

"Not exactly."

"You do have balls, Feegan, I'll give you that."

"Aw, jeez, Hayden. What's one drink gonna hurt, huh?"

"Feegan, how should I put this … we won't be meeting for a drink."

"See, now I kinda thought you might react that way, Hayden. But what would you say if I told you that the man you've been working for is way deep into something he shouldn't be. Doesn't that concern you?"

"What concerns me, Feegan, is that I've already spent too much time chatting with you tonight. Goodnight."

"But Hayden …"

Feegan's voice faded out as Hayden hung up the phone. Part of Hayden wanted to meet Feegan for that drink, to come clean on what appeared to be a charade over at Cheyenne, but Hayden didn't know anything. If Feegan had the goods on Aaron, he'd have to find someone else to help him do his homework.

Chapter 53

A six-man Delta team made its way to Sana'a. The
Pentagon had given the Yemeni government a vague heads-
up that something was going to go down, which the
Yemenis, eager to make nice with the U.S. after the
bombing of the USS Cole and 9/11, had accepted. The
Yemenis were in the midst of internal reform and were
determined not to let the country become a terrorist haven
like Afghanistan.

A blinding midday sun bounced off white gypsum
buildings in the ancient city. Midway down Sameer Street
stood a house, not unlike all the other houses. This is where
the Delta team was holed up. The facade was burnt brick
and stone. On the bottom floor was a tobacconist's shop run
by a small family named Al-Anisi

The family lived above the shop. Like their neighbors
they raised kids, made a living, and thanked Allah for what
they had. Unlike their neighbors, they were on the CIA's
payroll.

A good chunk of the family's pay came in the form of
an educational meal ticket for their son and daughter, who
had been sent to study in the United States.

On the third floor, above the aroma of sweet tobacco
from the store and saltah from the Al-Anisi kitchen, lived
Agent Bill Tully. Sameer Street was a convincing charade.
The Al-Anisi family went about their lives, didn't ask
questions and left Tully to come and go through a door

behind the counter in the store.

Chapter 54

It started with a crackle on his telephone line. Then there was the young red-headed woman that he had noticed not only in the square near his home but also on the tram, as well as on his regular Sunday walks along the lake in Seefeld. But maybe he was paranoid.

Jagmetti was certain that he was being followed. But by whom? He had tussled with the Swiss Federal Banking Authority (the EBK) once before, but they were up front about their investigations. They didn't sneak around. If he was under scrutiny for some reason, they would have made that plain by letter. He had received no such letter. Jagmetti's mind turned to the Russians. They liked to take things into their own hands. But if the Russians had a problem with him, they would have just told him to his face. That was the way they were. That left either MI6 or the CIA, or both. Jagmetti could not tell which one it was. Once upon a time, Jagmetti had taken on an IRA gun runner as a client. The guy would buy his wares in South Africa and run them through Antwerp, where they would be transported north to help "The Cause."

It wasn't particularly illegal for Jagmetti to have a gun runner as a client, as long as Jagmetti wasn't aware that his client was a gun runner, which, of course, he was, but then again, how could he be sure? And so, when the MI6 boys paid Jagmetti a visit to talk about it, he told them what they wanted to hear—that he was "absolutely stunned," and "how could this be?" Jagmetti agreed to terminate the man's account and thanked the MI6 agents for bringing the "very serious matter" to his attention.

This time felt a little different though. MI6 and the CIA had become quite skittish since 9/11. They had lost all sense of the irony or playfulness that they had during the Cold War. When it came to the war on terrorism, they weren't fooling around.

Jagmetti narrowed it down to the Client who was so keen to know when a communications satellite would be launched over Europe. He picked up his phone to make a call, but paused to remind himself that his phone was probably tapped. He put the receiver down, grabbed his and headed downstairs to a payphone on the square, the only place he felt he could speak freely. His lawyers would know what to do. He trusted them to know what to do. More important, he paid them to know what to do.

It was a bit chilly outside. Hayden was glad to have the warmth of the car. He saw Jagmetti leave his building and make his way to a pay phone. Jagmetti spoke for about three minutes and then left on foot. Hayden got out of the car.

The building had a key card system to enter. No worries, Benbow had set him up. Hayden pulled the card from his wallet and passed it over the card reader. The door clicked. In.

Hayden took the stairs, three floors to Jagmetti's office. Again, a card reader; again he entered.

The guy's office was clean. Hayden made his way to

the safe. Knowing that Jagmetti would recognize any changes to the contents of the safe, even the most minute, Hayden took painstaking care probing the files for what he was looking for. Once he found it, he took the paper out and placed it on Jagmetti's desk. He pulled out a miniature digital camera and began to take photos.

Twenty minutes had passed. He was pushing it, but the material was so good. He delicately replaced the paper back in the safe exactly where he had found it. Hayden could hear the elevator in the hallway. Someone was coming up.

Dammit, Hayden whispered to himself. He closed the safe door and made his way to the front of the office. No good. The elevator had stopped on his floor.

Chapter 55

Thankfully, it had been someone from another office who had gotten out of the elevator. Hayden was able to get out of Jagmetti's office undetected and make his way down the stairs to the street.

Back in his hotel room, Hayden lay on the bed, staring at the ceiling. He was still a bit jet lagged. He stood up, went into the bathroom and splashed cold water on his face. He went into the bedroom and sat down at his computer. He thought he would catch a few news headlines. He scanned his usual sites. Then he saw it, a lead story in *Fortune* magazine's online edition written by Thomas Feegan:

Cannondale's Folly: Why the World's Sixth Richest Man Invested in an Unknown Dutch Company, and Why You Shouldn't.

The article followed the usual pattern: build the person up to appear infallible, then let him have it. And because Aaron's childhood and adulthood were in such stark contrast to each other, the story made for great reading.

Feegan went into intimate detail about how Aaron's father had been a frustrated soul in a new country that he thought he understood, but really didn't. Feegan also talked about Aaron's mother, about how she was loving, but always conscious that she was living in a household with two men whose intellects were much more developed than her own. Feegan cited Aaron's motivations: wealth, influence, and power—exactly the three ingredients that Feegan and the magazine needed to transform Aaron from Horatio Alger to Gordon Gekko in less than 3,000 words.

As a speechwriter, Hayden understood the negative effect that raw ambition had on an audience, and he, therefore, instructed his clients to avoid it like kryptonite. As a journalist, Feegan understood the pejorative impact that ambition had on readers and, therefore, exposed it at every possible level.

Hayden had a hard time reading the entire article. He whispered to himself. *I told Aaron to keep his distance from Feegan.* Sentence after sentence, paragraph after paragraph were filled with the kind of venom normally reserved for mass murderers or dictators. And the words were backed up by plenty of numbers quantifying the ineptness of Cheyenne, the self-enriching relationship between Teestone Financial and Timmermans and Michelle, and the misfortune that would befall Cheyenne's innocent employees, many of whom were likely to lose their jobs.

Jesus, Michelle. Why did you have to go and do that? he thought to himself. She had been right to expect the worst, and it didn't get much worse than this. They would go after her. She had the keys to the treasure chest.

Hayden felt sick. She had been so tender with him, so selfless. He wished that she had come to him sooner before she had compromised herself, but that was history now.

Hayden read on. Cheyenne was profitless and buried under a mountain of debt. Worse, its principals couldn't articulate when or if it would ever be in the black. They challenged any analyst or market watcher who challenged them. According to Feegan's article, in one interview Timmermans apparently told a respected stock analyst in New York to "quit being so naive and join the future." Under normal circumstances, that particular foot in the mouth would have been followed by a slap from the analyst in the form of a reduced stock rating or a negative report. But that didn't happen. Feegan pointed to this as a sign that history was indeed repeating itself, that only a few years after the fall, the impatient principals at Cheyenne, determined to single-handedly get the tech market back on its feet, had successfully hoodwinked investors and persuaded analysts to go along for the ride—analysts who should have known better. And they went along because of two men. One of them was Cannondale. People listened to him because he epitomized success and, of course, because success was supposed to breed success.

The other person was less a man than a cult. The cult of Braun had emerged from the dot.com flames relatively intact. After the overcast market of the last few years, people desperately wanted to believe that Braun had changed, that the Street had changed, but as Feegan aptly said in his piece, "Greed, apparently, has no sell-by date."

Hayden shook his head. *Feegan has them.* Feegan had placed Timmermans' hand deep in the corporate cookie jar, exposing his penchant for expensive clothes, luxury cars, and fast deals with Russian satellite thugs who came off as menacing silhouettes lurking around an anything goes, post-Communist land grab.

The article, and those that would follow, had a reluctant Michelle cooking the books to make Cheyenne look healthier than it was. Also, damning was Feegan's account of how Teestone enriched certain Cheyenne principals, save Peter. Not only was it problematic, but it was a bold, catch-me-if-you-can return to the dot.com days.

And off in the distance, pulling the strings from a strange French chateau high above Salt Lake City, was Aaron Cannondale. Feegan painted Aaron as an eccentric living so high above the income levels of mere mortals that the lack of oxygen to his brain had made him odd and inattentive.

But something was conspicuously absent from the article, something that would have made Feegan and his editors orgasmic if they had been able to connect the dots, and that was Aaron's involvement in the fiduciary misconduct at Cheyenne. Nowhere in the article did Feegan actually accuse Aaron of any real wrongdoing other than being aloof.

Where is it? Hayden said out loud, searching the article for the damning evidence. But it wasn't there. Hayden re-read the section where Feegan called Aaron "odd" and "inattentive":

"Cannondale is most comfortable surrounding himself with an eclectic mix of people at what he immodestly calls his 'cabin' in Utah. This cabin has 34 rooms, ten bathrooms, an entire glass façade and a Biblical

Garden in the middle. It is the same 'cabin' where
Cannondale enjoys entertaining guests with gimmicks
like full rodeos, or renting out the cast of Cirque du Soleil for
private shows. It is the same 'cabin' where Cannondale
retreated to play video games and count his billions while
Cheyenne burned through money."

Feegan couldn't directly connect Aaron to the
improprieties. He couldn't connect him to Braun's overly
optimistic analyst reports.

Indeed, Feegan could not pin anything illegal on
Aaron, so he did the next best thing—he painted him as a
sort of defrocked technology cleric whose following was
fading.

Hayden stopped reading. He thought of the
implications that the article would have on Cheyenne, on
Aaron, on Michelle. There would be more articles, plenty
more. And those articles would pry deeper and deeper until
Cannondale became the poster child for a new era of
corporate hedonism. Yep, Feegan had himself a whopper of
a story, and there was no amount of damage control that
Aaron or Timmermans could deploy to stop it.

Hayden picked up the phone. He needed to make the
call now, while the anger was still ripe.

Chapter 56

Aaron's assistant, Libby, answered on the second ring. "Libby, it's Hayden."

"Well, well, well. If it's not the mystery boy. How are you, Hayden?" She liked him.

Mystery boy? What the hell did that mean, Hayden thought.

"Hayden, he's been stomping around and having us call all over creation for you. He's taking it out on everyone else. Where are you, Hayden? I can't tell from the caller ID on the phone."

"Just took some time off, that's all."

"Well, I'd better put you through to him before he finds out I'm sitting here chatting with you."

"Thanks, Libby. Libby?"

"Yes, Hayden."

"Take care of yourself."

"I certainly will," Libby said, slightly disarmed by the tone of Hayden's voice. "Just a moment."

Hayden could just imagine the look on Aaron's face as Libby was telling him that "Hayden" was on the phone.

"Well, Hayden, you'd better have a good excuse. I've had my folks looking all over the place for you. Where the hell are you? Have you seen this *Fortune* magazine nonsense?"

"I'm helping a friend with a problem."

"Does your friend not have a phone?"

"Service is sporadic."

"Well, wherever the hell you are, I need you to get back here. This thing is a mess, and I've already got calls from the *Journal* and the *Times,* which I haven't returned."

"I'm not coming back, Aaron."

"You're … hold on a second, Hayden … Libby, tell those guys that I'll call them back. And … oh, Libby, cancel my lunch, will you? Sorry Hayden. What were you saying?"

"I said I'm not coming back, Aaron."

"Not coming back? What does that mean, not coming back?"

"It means you're going to have to find yourself another speechwriter. It means I can't do your book for you. It means I'm moving on."

Silence.

"What the hell are you talking about, Hayden? Quit playing games. I need you back here."

"I'm sorry, Aaron."

"Sorry? You're sorry? I take you in. I show you the inside. I introduce you to a world you were likely to have never seen, and all you can say is 'I'm sorry'? Well, that's not good enough, Hayden. That's not good enough at all."

"I don't like what I see, Aaron."

"You don't like what you see with what?"

"With Cheyenne, with Kuipers, the whole thing. It feels oily."

"Oily? Well, you can thank your lucky fucking stars

Hayden that you don't need to deal with such things. I guess you can take great satisfaction in knowing that you don't need to deal with the messy stuff, Hayden—the hard stuff. You can live your little Bohemian life and float in and out of people's lives with no strings attached and cast moral aspersions as far as the eye can see. That must be a nice gig, Hayden."

"I had hoped it wouldn't come to this, Aaron."

"Come to what, Hayden? Come to the six-inch knife that you've just stuck in my kidney? Is that what you're talking about, my friend? Whether you like it or not you're in. You're in up to your eyeballs, so don't think for a minute that you're just going to walk away."

"I'm out, Aaron."

"You're in, Hayden! Do you hear me? You're in. Don't you dare dump me. No one dumps me, you got that?"

"It was fun for a while, Aaron, but I don't believe in it any longer."

"I'm giving you five seconds to reconsider, Hayden. Five seconds. Five, four …"

Strangely, as Hayden listened to Aaron count down, he didn't feel the slightest pang of hesitation. He thought of how it once was—the parties at Aaron's home, those quiet moments when Aaron bared his soul. Then, his mind's eye turned to all the whispering in corners with the Teestone guys. And that scared look in Aaron's eye in the hotel lobby after the speech in Detroit.

"Three … two …"

Hayden was going to miss Aaron. He really was loved the kind of words that Aaron had let him put in his mouth. Once upon a time, Hayden had thought that everybody was really just the same. He no longer believed that.

" … One. Goodbye, Hayden."

Hayden heard the click on the other end. He paused.

"Goodbye, Aaron."

Chapter 57

Michelle had just quit. Her departure confirmed that something was very wrong at Cheyenne, even without the Feegan article.

Peter was now worth in excess of $27 million—more than enough to do just about anything that he wanted. And that evening in Amsterdam with a cup of tea by his side and Thelonious Monk's "Evidence" playing in the background, he decided exactly what he would do. He was going to quit, too.

"Quit?" Timmermans said, shocked. He was pacing around his office as Peter calmly sat in a chair. "Over one silly article?"

"It's not just the article, Phillipe. I've had enough."

"Enough of what?"

"Enough of this. I'm getting bored, Phillipe. Time to move on to something else."

"But we're not done yet, Peter. And we've got this damn problem with the satellite moving around up there. Who's going to take care of that?"

"I'm done."

"But we're just getting started, Peter."

"I've gotten you this far. The rest … well, the rest is up to you." Timmermans fumbled for his cigarette case in his coat

"What the hell am I going to tell Cannondale? He's going to go crazy."

273

"No, he's not. It will take him about five minutes to get over it, Phillipe."

"But we've been through so much together, Peter. Why now?"

"It's no longer fun, Phillipe. The whole thing has been turned over to the suits, and look at the mess they've gotten us into. I'm finished; I'm done."

"You're making a huge mistake, Peter."

"Maybe."

Phillipe shook his head. "What will you do?"

"What I've wanted to do for some time—buy a ranch, raise some cattle, take up with an American girl with big hair. It doesn't matter."

"I think you're crazy, Peter. I think you're absolutely nuts. We've only just begun to capture people's imagination about a world where time and space have no restrictions, a world where people can instantly communicate to anyone, anywhere on the planet in real time. Imagine that, Peter. Don't you want to be a part of that?"

"I will be a part of that somehow, Phillipe. It's inevitable. I just don't want to work at Cheyenne anymore."

Peter stood up and extended his hand. "Best of luck to you, Phillipe. Come visit."

With that, Peter walked out of Phillipe's office. He could hear the thud of Phillipe's fist hitting the desk as he left, but Peter's mind was already far away on a sylvan butte somewhere outside of Pinedale, Wyoming. He reached into his back pocket for the piece of paper that had been his touchstone since the first day he and Timmermans had talked about starting Cheyenne. He unfolded the paper:

"There's a place in the Wyoming mountains where time slows down, the air smells clean, the water runs pure, and the people are down-home friendly. Boulder Lake Lodge is truly at the 'end of the road,' nestled in the foothills of the Bridger National Forest. Thick aspen groves and pine-covered hillsides set the stage for one of the finest vacations in the Wind River Mountains."

Chapter 58

Hayden poured himself a bourbon on the rocks from the hotel mini-bar and sat at the desk to examine the documents that he had photographed in Jagmetti's office. Next to him was the tape machine that had captured Jagmetti's phone calls.

Jagmetti's records were pristine—dates, times, account numbers, phone numbers. Hayden wasn't sure what he was looking for, but he kept digging. He saw references to Timmermans and Peter at Cheyenne—dates and times of calls. He saw a complete log of the satellite deal with Riga-Tech. There was even a list of paintings that Jagmetti had purchased in the past two years.

Hayden paused. *That's odd.* It was a calendar entry. Jagmetti had apparently met with the European Commissioner for Competition, Sir Graham Eatwell. Nothing particularly strange about that, except that the subject of the meeting was listed as "Cheyenne/N-tel." What did N-tel, the Dutch telecom company, have to do with Cheyenne, and why was the European Commissioner for Competition meeting with a random Swiss banker about Cheyenne? Aaron and Timmermans would love to know about that little nugget.

Hayden rubbed his eyes and got up to pace around the room. He carried Jagmetti's calendar entries with him. There were several phone numbers. One of them caught Hayden's eye. Next to it Jagmetti had scribbled "satellite." How many satellite launches could Jagmetti be involved with? Hayden guessed not many. It must be related to Cheyenne. It was too coincidental. Besides, the entry dates were roughly around the same time that Cheyenne had purchased its satellite.

Hayden wrote down the number. He poured himself a little more bourbon and freshened up the ice. He began to listen to a few of Jagmetti's taped conversations. It started off innocently enough—a couple of women, an old friend, social calendar calls. One conversation between Jagmetti and Zlotkov was comical. The communications gap was clear. Each got increasingly louder and repetitive as the call progressed.

Another call intrigued Hayden for its venom toward the United States. Jagmetti was sharing his thoughts with a business partner on why a new world order was beginning to bloom.

Hayden half paid attention to the next call and then fast forwarded. He stopped himself. *That was kind of interesting.* The caller had only identified himself by a number, his Swiss bank account number. Hayden rewound.

It was the Client. Hayden didn't know it yet, but he had stumbled on Jagmetti's mysterious Client—the one that only identified himself by his account number.

Hayden picked up the man's accent immediately. It was Arabic. Hayden was good with dialects. The voice wasn't from the Maghreb. It wasn't from the Gulf. Egypt! The man was Egyptian. Jagmetti was kissing his ass on the call.

**"Hello. Oh yes, very good to hear from you,"
Jagmetti said. "It's quite pleasant in Zurich today,**

thank you very much. And how about by you? … I see. The satellite? Well, it is operating quite nicely, from what I understand. Well, thank you very much. Certainly … not a problem. My pleasure."

Hayden stopped the tape. He looked at the date of the call. *Cheyenne,* he thought to himself. *They've got to be talking about Cheyenne. But why is the Egyptian interested?* Hayden had no recollection of an Egyptian being involved with Cheyenne's satellite deal. It had been all Riga-Tech. Hayden's mind wandered. *Why an Egyptian?* Doesn't make sense.

Words like "satellite," "GPS," "Russians," and "Kuipers" rolled around in his head. And then "GPS" and "Adirondacks." Hayden remembered the news article that he kept in his speechwriting folder. He rushed to his leather workbag and fished for it. There it was. The piece pointed out that the signal coming from certain satellites travels 11,000 miles, so weak that by the time it arrived on Earth a single Christmas tree light was about 1,000 times as bright. The article went on to say that the signal could essentially be altered by anyone possessing a jamming device that they could get off the Internet for $40.

Hayden's eyes widened. *Jagmetti was in on it. Or he was a stooge. The Arab wanted to know when the satellite was going up so that they could hack into it! That's how they knew. That's how they were able to time it. That's why I walked off a ridge in the Adirondacks. That's why special forces guys were accidentally calling in air strikes on themselves.*

Hayden's mind raced. He looked at his watch and then reached for the phone.

There was a long pause. Then Benbow. "It's me. I can't talk on this line. Switch over to email. I need you to look into something immediately."

"Got it," Benbow said, hanging up.

Hayden turned to his computer, which was equipped with an encrypted email system. He began to type:

(Hayden) Been listening to our friend's phone calls here in Zurich.

(Benbow) Good.

(Hayden) He told them.

(Benbow) Told who? What?

(Hayden) Whoever hacked into the satellite before it went up. Jagmetti told them when it would be launched.

There was a long pause before Benbow responded. Hayden could tell that he was digesting the information.

(Benbow) You sure?

(Hayden) Pretty sure. Can you trace a Swiss bank account number?

(Benbow) Not without some phone calls to the Swiss. Will take at least 24 hours.

(Hayden) It'll be worth your while. Here's the number. He's Egyptian. Find him and you'll find the money funding the GPS problem.

(Benbow) Is our friend still in Zurich?

(Hayden) Yes.

(Benbow) Keep an eye on him.

(Hayden) Of course.

Hayden logged off, turned off the lights in the room, and walked onto the balcony. The sky was full of stars, and a satellite or two.

Chapter 59

Hayden's cell phone was ringing as he entered his hotel room. He had just been out for a run.

"Hello?"

"He panned out," Benbow

"The Egyptian?"

"Yep. He's been on our list. Not a nice guy. He's well-connected in the region, including Yemen."

"Not surprising."

"No, but it's one less ghost out there to chase."

"What happens next?"

"If the Egyptians play ball, they'll pick him up, but not until Delta does what it needs to do in Yemen."

"And Jagmetti?"

"Same story, although the Swiss will do it quietly."

Hayden couldn't help but think that once the headlines started flowing linking terrorism and Cheyenne, it would be the beginning of the end for the company. The principals had done nothing wrong on that front. How were they to know that terrorists had hacked into their satellite, but with attention would come increased scrutiny. It wasn't going to happen for him and Michelle. He felt helpless. Damn, he was going to miss her.

"Ok, Benbow, you need me right now?"

"You got something better to do?"

"Yeah, I need to take a shower."

Chapter 60

Graham Eatwell craved a nice cup of tea.

Tea—the great soother. Tea—the detoxifier and demulcent; the transporter of time, the talisman of thought.

How odd, Eatwell thought, that the sober act of boiling drinking water as a hygienic precaution in China 5,000 years ago would one day lead to the unrestrained practice of tea drinking—lots of tea, every day in great quantities by large populations around the world.

How heroic of the Portuguese Jesuit Father Jasper de Cruz to filter tea in 1560 from the Orient to Europe, where it would sell for over $100 per pound.

How absolutely civilized of the Dutch in the 17th century to make tea a fixture of taverns, inns, and restaurants.

How very American it had been for the smallish colony of New York, tea drinkers since Peter Stuyvesant and consuming more tea at one time than all of England put together, to eventually give in to the corruption of coffee.

The brown liquid warmed Eatwell's insides and steadied his nerves. He felt lightheaded, as if he was going to be sick. And yet, he could not turn away from the TV.

The backdrop was a snowy Zurich. Jagmetti had been arrested. His alleged crime: aiding and abetting the terrorists that had hacked into Cheyenne's satellite.

It was not a small indiscretion. And the Swiss authorities, no doubt under tremendous pressure from the Americans, were going to great lengths to make an example of Jagmetti. Financial sins were normally taken care of discretely in Europe. Not this time. Someone in Washington had made a call to someone in Switzerland to demand that Jagmetti be given the full treatment.

Jagmetti's crime was indefensible. He would fall hard, and his rolodex, and all of the names in it, would become the subject of great intrigue. Eatwell shook his head. How had his friend Kuipers, his dear friend Kuipers, led him to such a man?

Eatwell took a sip of his tea and cleared his throat as if he was about to say something, but there was nothing to say, nor anyone to say it to. Derek was in Antwerp for the weekend visiting friends. Bernard asked for the night off to take care of his aging mother. Eatwell, of course, let him go, but not before having him draw a bath. Eatwell had defended Europe, and for that he felt proud. Cheyenne had introduced a revolutionary technology to the world under his watch. But what a pyrrhic victory it had been. Hundreds of Cheyenne's employees—Europeans—were about to find themselves jobless. A perfectly beautiful, homegrown technology had been soiled.

Yes, the American press painted Cannondale as a greed merchant, but it was also palpably pleased to throw what it characterized as European immorality into the mix. To make matters worse, the bargain that Eatwell had struck with Jagmetti was predicated on the understanding that Jagmetti would get information about Cheyenne's technology into N-tel's hands, yet there was little evidence that N-tel was making any effort to capitalize on it, at least from what Eatwell could tell. They seemed incapable of getting out of their own way.

What a waste. For all the risks that Eatwell had taken, for all the intellectual dishonesty that he had indulged in for the greater good of Europe, there were few signs that his efforts had altered much of anything. Cannondale was still rich, Europe was still playing catch-up, and America was still on top.

Eatwell finished his tea and set the mug down on the coffee table. His eye caught his father and mother looking back at him from a photo on the desk across the room. They were 22 when the picture of them was taken in the Lake District—so young, so optimistic. They had prepared him well for this world, and he had made them proud.

Eatwell walked to the bathroom and slipped off his robe. The sight of his sagging body in the mirror made him shake his head. He had never felt completely comfortable in it.

The smell of eucalyptus oil was intense. He always had Bernard add an extra capful when he drew the bath. Eatwell put his big toe in the water and pulled it back. *Perfect.*

Next to the tub was a low, wooden table upon which Eatwell normally placed a cup of tea or a book. Not tonight. Tonight, he wanted to listen to the BBC World Service. He took the radio from the sink counter and drew the cord out, placing the radio on the table.

The heat in the water caused Eatwell to hold his breath

for a second as he submerged his body. He loved that sensation. It reminded him of being a kid, of making that first leap of the summer season into the deep lake where they had always gone on holiday. He thought of his parents again, and of all the things he would have liked to have done.

Eatwell turned on the radio. They were playing the best of Alistair Cooke, who had died a few years back. He was delivering one of his Letters from America, as he had done with great affection since 1946. The older Cooke grew, the more his Letters wandered, but that didn't bother Eatwell. It was the voice and the cadence, and the odd connections that Cooke made that had always hypnotized him.

Cooke talked about baseball and postage stamps and the particularly American pursuit of reinventing oneself. But it wasn't reinvention that Eatwell was interested in when he took the radio from the table with his wet hands and placed it in the tub with him. He had no intention of coming back as anything. There wasn't much dignity in dying in the bathtub, but that's where they would find him—naked, wet, and full of electricity.

Chapter 61

The intercept in Yemen that Bill Tully had originally passed on to Benbow had come from a house in Sana'a that Tully affectionately called "Starbucks," in honor of Yemen's coffee history. This is where Nabil and Hassan were doing their damage.

The Delta force was now in place. It was led by Captain Robbie Duran and filled out by guys named Velaquez, Polen, Agee and Sheridan.

Benbow and Hayden were together back in Virginia, connected by satellite feed into the Delta Team's ear pieces. Duran's call sign for this mission was "Osprey39." Benbow's call sign was "Gopher10."

"Gopher10, this is Osprey39. We can hear you." The Delta guys were on the ground floor of Starbucks.

"What the hell was that?" one of the soldiers said in the mic.

"A horse, sir."

It was Tulsa, the horse that Nabil and Hassan kept on the ground floor of Starbucks. Just then, another one of the soldiers chimed in. He and two others were on higher floors of the house.

"No one is here, sir."

"Osprey39, this is Gopher 10. What, pray tell?" Benbow said in disbelief.

"Somebody must have tipped them off. It looks like they left in a hurry."

"Are the computers still there?" Benbow asked, frustrated.

"They are."

"Proceed. Get in there."

Chapter 62

Two PCs sat side-by-side on a wooden table. Captain Duran put down his gun and sat at the table. He was a gifted computer guy, and he was about to demonstrate why.

Not too far away, in the diwan of a house within eyesight of Starbucks, a small boy drank tea and ate dates with his father and brothers, never speaking a word of the two strangers who gave him a handful of rials to keep watch for foreigners around Starbucks while playing with his friends in the street.

"I don't like it," Duran said.

"Me neither," barked Benbow.

"Get to that keyboard."

Polen walked into the room. He looked Duran in the eye and gave the thumbs up. Apparently they had found a sniper on the roof. The sniper was now dead.

"There's a back door," someone said through the ear pieces. Duran started pointing.

"Take posts."

Duran stared at the screen. It was hard to know where to begin.

He cleared his throat to speak.

"Gopher10, Opsrey39. Ready?" Duran asked.

"Roger that, Osprey39."

"Give me a minute to take a look at this," Duran said.

They had rehearsed this. Duran had neither the time nor the ability to single-handedly undo what Nabil and Hassan had done. His instructions were clear: uncover the computer files that were affecting Cheyenne's satellite, FTP the files to Langley's servers, and get the hell out of there. Once the download was complete, the Agency programmers would then handle the backbreaking work of slicing and dicing the code, and fixing what was broken.

Benbow turned the line over to the programmers. "Go ahead, Osprey39."

Duran began identifying and batching the relevant files in the directories. He scrolled through folders and subfolders with names like cmd_ctrl_propulsion, cmd_ctrl_attitude, and cmd_ctrl_comm. Polen kept peering out the window. Agee looked around downstairs. Velaquez was on the roof. Sheridan remained on the perimeter somewhere around the house.

Duran typed in ftp.hermit.gov. The computer paused until connected to ftp.hermit.gov appeared on the screen. Duran typed in his login: "Osprey39," and then the password: "JerryAb2Jeff." Again, there was another pause until "User Osprey Logged In" appeared on the screen.

"Alright," Duran said out loud, somewhat surprised that it was actually working. "One more step," he said in his microphone.

"Good stuff, Ospey39. Just FTP us the batched files and you'll be on your way."

Duran saw the FTP prompt, cracked his knuckles, typed in the string and hit Return. An hourglass appeared on the screen.

"Hang tight, Osprey39. It's gonna take a few minutes for the download to complete."

"No problem," Duran said.

Just then, Velaquez heard what sounded like a piece of fruit smacking against the stone next to him on the roof. It was no fruit. It was a Russian grenade. Velaquez's eyes widened. He ran to the other side of the small roof. The blast occurred just as he flung himself onto the rope that he had used to climb up.

The house shook. Velaquez clung to the rope. He checked himself out. He was fine, at least until the bullet from a Kalashnikov ripped into his thigh. He lost his grip and fell about 10 feet to the ground in a heap of pain.

The explosion had blown a hole in the roof of the fourth story, but it hadn't damaged the ceiling of the third floor where Duran was working the computers. There was an eerie pause, and then a hail of bullets. Duran hit the floor. Polen was in the corner near the window barking something into his mic. Duran positioned himself behind a chair.

The bullets seemed to come from multiple directions. They zipped through the air, ricocheting off the stone walls. As suddenly as it had started, the volley stopped.

The download! Hayden thought. He spoke into his mic. His call sign for the mission was Corona17. "Osprey39, Osprey39, this is Corona17, are you there?"

"Affirmative."

"Get that download!"

"Working on it." Duran crept up from the floor to see the hourglass on the screen. *A third full. Dammit.*

"Velaquez is hit, sir," Hayden could hear one of the soldiers, Sheridan he thought, telling Duran.

"Gopher 10, we have one down."

Duran could hear Sheridan's M4 from the perimeter of the house. He could also hear men shouting in Arabic. Once again, he inched up the table to the PCs to check the hourglass. *Half full. Shit, this thing is slow.*

Another hail of bullets. None of this was supposed to be happening. It was a first-class set-up.

Polen was getting instructions from someone about a sniper's whereabouts outside. He put on his night vision goggles and rolled onto the floor under the window sill. He moved up the wall until his head was just beneath the window, pausing to find the right moment. He inched the barrel of his M4 out the open window, paused again, then fired.

"No more sniper," Hayden could hear Polen say. Duran typed furiously, trying his best to speed up the hourglass.

"How we doing, Ospey39?" Benbow asked Duran.

"Hourglass is three-quarters full."

Benbow looked at Hayden in the command room at Langley as if to say, "What do you think?" Hayden shook his head.

"Done!" Duran shouted. "We're out of here. Gopher10, we are evacuating. Repeat. We are evacuating."

The shooting started again. Duran hit the floor. Polen

and the others returned fire. There was a long pause in all of their headsets.

"Roger that. Pull out," Hayden could hear someone saying to Duran.

As Duran and Polen descended the stairs in the house, Agee rushed, knocking them backwards. Someone had tossed a grenade through the main floor window. The explosion blew the front doors of the house off. Hayden could hear some of the soldiers choking on the dust. Duran spoke to Sheridan on his headset.

"Okay, guys. We're going out the back."

They would pick up Velaquez on the way out. He was still pinned down behind some trash. Polen went out first. He kept low, and then dove next to Velaquez on the ground. Velaquez's leg was a mess. No way could he walk. Agee went out next, bee-lined straight up a small hill and hid behind the crumbling wall of a nearby house. Duran was still inside the house. He counted to three, then sprinted to help Polen with Velaquez. Duran crouched over Velaquez, his back to the house. Agee could see a figure slowly appear in the doorway. The man would have taken out Duran, Polen, and Velaquez if Agee hadn't pumped five rounds into the man's chest. The figure slumped to the ground.

Duran pulled Velaquez over his shoulder and made a run for it while Polen covered his rear. The return fire weakened. It was hard to tell how many people were shooting at them.

"I count four of theirs down," Hayden could hear

Sheridan say over the headset. He was near the front door. "Possibly four left." Duran leaned Velaquez against the wall. Their Toyota pickup was parked across the street.

"Agee, you and Polen get Velaquez into the truck," Duran was shouting. "Gentlemen, hold fire for a moment. Let's see how cocky these guys are."

Duran could just make out their shapes in the interior of the house. He steadied his gun. "Come on … come on …" he said, waiting for the right moment. He fired. Two more dead guys.

Sheridan quickly made his way to Duran and the others in the back of the house. They caught their breath and then bolted for the truck. Agee fired up the engine. They piled in and drove off as quickly as they had come. Hayden could only imagine the relief that the team was feeling as they drove away.

Chapter 63

A group of kids threw snowballs as Hayden emerged from the subway exit.

"Come on," they said, pleading with him to play. He put his backpack down, made a couple of snowballs and let them have it. The kids went wild. Hayden smiled. He was tired, too tired to sleep so he decided to get some air. The walk across the Brooklyn Bridge gave him time to readjust to the sounds and smells of New York. He felt at home in a way that his life had never allowed him to feel about a place. Midway across the bridge, he paused to look at the Statue of Liberty. His gaze drifted to the right toward the place once known as Ground Zero. He breathed in deeply—a mixture of salt air and gasoline from the cars buzzing beneath him. He closed his eyes for a moment. When he opened them, it was as if something had clicked. The images of the powdered faces running north, of the gaping hole in the South Tower, of bodies raining down on the pavement were gone. Surprisingly, what remained was the color of the sky, the brilliant blue of that crisp September morning.

Hayden had thought that the benevolence of the sky had been stripped away from him, that the menace that lurked high among the clouds, behind the cloak of blue, would linger forever. But it hadn't. It all depended on the light in which you viewed it. His thoughts turned to what he'd do next. He had a lead in Washington with the senior senator from North Carolina. He had also received a call from one of the leading diplomats at the UN. But what he really wanted to do for the time being was nothing at all.

He took a cab back to his apartment. He threw his things down, went to the kitchen sink, turned on the faucet, and splashed cold water on his face. He flicked on his CD player and put in an old Neil Young album that he hadn't listened to in ages. He smiled as he heard the first few chords of "Emperor of Wyoming." It made him wonder if Peter had made it out to Wyoming yet—out there in the fresh air and open space and streams brimming with fish.

He grabbed an Amstel Light out of the refrigerator and turned on the TV to find some news. When he got to C-Span, he grinned a knowing grin. Standing there, delivering a speech before a packed crowd at the St. Francis in San Francisco, was Aaron. The audience was hypnotized. Despite the headlines and the scandals, they still wanted to hear what the sixth richest man in the world had to say.

Hayden noticed an entranced guy in the front row. A woman to the side nodded her head in agreement. They were his. Aaron had them. And for a brief moment in time, he'd had Hayden, too.

- End -

Epilogue

Cheyenne imploded—another casualty of an American economy that had increasingly become reliant on wing walking from bubble to bubble to sustain itself. Hayden couldn't help but wonder if anyone at Cheyenne had thought to call the guy who had shown up at one of Aaron's parties—the guy who bought used office furniture and equipment from failed start-ups.

* * * *

Jagmetti didn't spend any time in jail. Neither the U.S. nor the Swiss authorities were able to make a strong case regarding his tenuous relationship with the Egyptian, who had disappeared. Jagmetti reunited with his clients. He still has lunch at Cantinella Antinori in the old town near St. Peter's Church in Zurich, and he still orders the veal.

* * * *

Graham Eatwell's death was eventually deemed a suicide. Despite his vast network of friends and contacts, his funeral was not well attended. Derek sat in the back of the church, tears in his eyes, keeping his distance for fear of outing Graham even after his death. The European Commission put up a plaque in Eatwell's honor. "For his incalculable efforts in fashioning a Europe prosperous and at peace," it said.

* * * *

Timmermans and Michelle were found guilty of securities fraud. They sit in male and female prisons 60 kilometers from each other in the Netherlands. Michelle's boat, *Wavelength*, is still docked in Amsterdam. A friend lives on it. Timmermans' wife divorced him. When he can get them, he still smokes Dunhill blues.

* * * *

Braun's reputation was nicked, but he was not severely injured. The financial press beat him up a bit for his positive treatment of Cheyenne. Federal regulators, consumed with other matters, didn't pile on the way they had earlier in this decade. The speculation was that they didn't want to play that movie reel again and that they viewed Cheyenne as merely a delayed Dutch version of the dot.com fiasco in the U.S. Teestone didn't fare as well. It had fines slapped on it. Vaughn retired to North Carolina.

* * * *

Volskov's military peers were angry that he had drawn undue attention the fact that many of them were moonlighting to make money on the side. A couple of them agreed not to make his life difficult if he cut them in on future satellite deals. Zlotnikov and Tebelis were never fingered for Kuipers' death. Zlotnikov was on his own now. Tebelis had been found in one of his nightclubs, shot through the head assassination style—a victim of Russian mob turf wars.

* * * *

Benbow won praise within the Agency for his handling of the satellite episode. When he's not teaching at The Farm, he takes in minor league baseball games.

* * * *

Cannondale just sold his home in Bermuda and is dating one of the judges on American Idol.

* * * *

Feegan, the journalist, has stepped up his alcohol intake and has his own blog.

* * * *

Hayden took some time off for a long overdue return trip to Morocco. He is entertaining writing gigs.

* * * *

Peter lives on a spread in the Wind River Valley in Wyoming with his girlfriend, Tammy. They have two black labs and a 1979 Ford Lariat F-150 pickup. On Fridays, he fishes for browns and cutthroat. He still loves everything about water.

Author Bio

Angus Morrison is a Pulitzer-nominated, former financial journalist for Bloomberg, and has contributed to *The International Herald Tribune, The New York Observer* and the *Globalist*. He was a speechwriter for the U.S. Secretary of State and IBM's senior executive suite, and served as Senior Policy Advisor at the U.S. State Department. He lives with his wife and son in Paris.

In college, he flipped hamburgers and fixed fences in Wyoming. After graduation, he moved to Brussels where he lived in a nun's cell in a former convent that had been converted into communal living quarters. In his free time, he frequented a small Flemish pub that counted a large black Bouvier named "Zeus" as its most loyal patron.

The Berlin Wall fell while Morrison was in Brussels. He hitchhiked to Budapest in 26 vehicles. The first thing he saw upon arrival in Hungary were Cold War statues torn down as the communist star was being wrenched off the parliament by a crane.